NEW-CL _ _ _ _ _ S

BOOK SIX

CONTINUUM

TREVOR WATTS

Continuum Copyright © 2022 by Trevor Watts.

All rights reserved. No part of this book may be reproduced in any form or by any electronic or mechanical means including information storage and retrieval systems, without permission in writing from the author. The only exception is by a reviewer, who may quote short excerpts in a review.

This book is a work of fiction. Names, characters, places, and incidents either are products of my imagination or are used fictitiously. Any resemblance to actual persons, living or dead, events, or locales is entirely because I have, in the past seventy-odd years met thousands of people, and travelled through almost a hundred countries, and I can barely separate real memories from imagination sometimes. The illustrations were all created by me or adapted from free-to-download, or paid-for, images from the internet.

Dedicated to Chris Watts
For her editing skills, commitment and tolerance.
Log on to www.sci-fi-author.com
and www.trevorwattsauthor.co.uk
Facebook at Creative Imagination
First Printing: 2022
Brinsley Publishing Services

ISBN: 9798747669208

Contents

A BIT BIGGER.	1
WARPHANS	9
EFFO	18
THEY'RE ONLY HUMANS	31
SOMETHING TO BE DONE	39
CONTINUUM	63
JUST VISITING	69
CHITS	77
BREACH: LEVEL 2	93
AND TIME GNAWED BY.	101
CHOICES	107
KALEIDOSCOPE	123
JUST SOME OLD GUY	131
THE EMPEROR'S NEW CLOTHES	135
A BIT OF BOTHER	153
MY WIFE HAS THE FATTEST BACKSIDE	165
WHO STARTED THE WAR?	167
ME, PROF AND A TAIL TO TELL	185
I'M NOT PERFECT YET	195
ROMANCE ON THE ROCKS	199
A few notes	217
The Author and his Books	220

A BIT BIGGER.

'Give it a rest, lads. *Give it a skagging rest!*'

I only heard cos the power went off and my yakker-chisel seized.

'Shift's over.' Boss Sydun was there, his over-drags still clean. So he'd only just come underground, and his first thing was to cut power to my chiz. Stupid.

Shift being over was kayho with me, but we shouldn't stop just like that – my chiz jammed solid in the rock. It's spud-near as big as I am, and just as heavy. The sonic-vibro-tip ought to be extracted slow and careful, not left in there. It'll have gone solid the instant it stopped; bonded with the rock. That molib bit costs three days' pay. Not out my account, it doesn't come. I'll tell him if he tries that on. My auto-log'll have it recorded.

'So what's up?' I asked him, thinking that restarting the solid-jammed chiz would put all the torque through the motor instead of the bit-point. It'd either twist, and warp the whole mechanism; or break my wrists, and throw me across the cave we've spent eight days digging and blasting out. Probably both, then it'd all be useless.

'Got another job for you, Kurdi. Now.'

Ah, shuvvit; no deep matter to me. I don't have shares in the mine, or the yakker-chisel, or even in this vein of mercurium. It's been a shygger so far: it's mixed with gallirium, and that's a blend from the furnace of Hellas. It's so hard we need the molib-diamond tips on the full 18GHz to eat into it.

'Stop fretting. We'll get it out from the side, later,' he said. He reads minds, you'd think, the way he does that.

But he's right: it'd be cheaper to do that than disconnect the bit and abandon it in the rockface.

As the best gang on the planet – such as it is – we extract more of the stuff per octo than any other unit. And, as I'm the gang's Shiftman, that makes me and my arm just as valuable as the yakker-machine.

'Outside undertaking, Kurdi. Somewhat different. Triple wages for a single shift. Bring the 240xx with you. With the rack of vibro-bits. Couple of diamond chisel boosters; and double-capacity cables. Get them loaded in a trolley-trailer. Plus spare work suits; reinforced gloves; whatever you think for a tough job.'

So I'm wondering what the Yeck is going on while we go back up the shaft, most-of-a-shift earlier than usual. 'Special job, then, Bossman?'

No answer.

*

It was still dark when we arrived at the entrance to Hades Mine. I always pause a moment in gratitude to Ragath for safe re-delivery to the surface. Both moons up and almost full. One slightly blue-tinged; the other more yellow, but smaller. We filled a half-trailer with extra equipment at the stores shack, and loaded it all behind an HD cab, and he was saying, 'It's to do the same kind of chisel and chop job as you're on now.'

'But?' There was obviously a "but" if it was triple wages.

'It's on the t'neetas.'

'The t'neetas?' I laughed. 'You're pulling me off this to dig out some old bones in a cliff face? Where? Out at Rozny? The bone cliff?'

That's where the t'neetas are found. A hundred kiks high, the cliff is supposedly partly made of some vast ancient creatures' ribs or something.

'Near there, yes; a bit further, beyond Rozny. Better bring a selection of bits – some of the rotary ones. Couple of side-swipers. And a Shatter-all. Booster packs? Okay? Come on.'

*

Two hours to get there, to the cliff.

'They are sure impressive, if you're into that kind of thing – former life-forms on this planet,' I agreed, looking across at this cliff face where a crew had had a go at chiselling out the maybe-ribs. Some time back, that was, when somebody was making a play for a tourist industry, when we were new on Halcya. Now, these things are like white curved trees up the face of the cliff, etched into a stronger relief.

'Know much about the t'neetas, Kurdi?'

I shrugged, 'Fossils from before The Scorching; long before humans arrived here. They do look like they could be ribs. But who cares? We're not going to carve them out? What? we're archaeologists now? Geologists? Paleontol—'

'Can you imagine how big a live one must have been?'

I thought about it. 'If they crawled? Mmm. A bit higher than the cliff?'

'Weighing around a million and a half gK. Twenty-thousand times bigger than you, or me.'

'You've spent time out here, then, Boss?' I said, just to make conversation, 'Learning all this?'

'Research team approached us just recently, for help with their project. Come on, I'll show you the latest ones they've found.'

*

'Actually,' Sydun said, as we rounded a bluff the best part of an hour further on, 'the team discovered several together. A sort of colony. A nest of them; twenty-odd years ago. And they've been studying them.'

We paused for a moment for another cab and trailer to come past the other way. I glanced back, into all the gear we had stacked up in our trailer. It was a formidable collection of everything from mini-blasters to HD vibro-tip drill bits.

'These t'neetas, Kurdi, it seems they're dying. Solidifying or something—'

'They're *what?* Dying? *They're alive?*'

'For the time being, but they almost totally lack mobility now. Practically fossilising from the inside, they reckon. Come on, round here.'

*

'Ah gentlemen.' As we pulled up in the trailer-cab, this older official-type greeted us. 'Come see the size of the job.'

He led us through these high tight-mesh gates to a viewpoint over a small valley. Seven, maybe eight, I counted, of these things, like lizargars, but with big eyes. 'They're longer than the tunnel we're digging.'

He looked at us, this old official guy, and led us down among these things – the t'neetas. And close-up, yes, they were cliff-sized.

'Absolutely scooging huge.' I was staring up at them, and I got the feeling they were eyeing me up for dinner as we went round. It was like they were made of rock, but you could see lines, like creases, so there must be some movement possible.

'That's the head, is it?' I asked when we came to an enormous bulbous part where the eyes were perched on the top. Like half a cliff above my head.

'The head? Indeed it is. And here's the problem; they're getting some metallic mineral growths in their orifices. We believe these crystals are preventing them ingesting food, which appears to be the dense oil-shale rocks down the far end of the valley.'

'And we're supposed to? What? De-plaque their teeth?'

'You got the idea,' he says, and starts scraping a long pole against the side of the head, up near one eye.

'Jips! That's a mouth?' This cavern opened up. Twice the height of our cabin, revealing a crystalline mass that was practically filling the whole maw. Through the bulk of the massed crystals, I could see white columns rising. The tips of them did, anyway.

'If those columns are teeth, then, yes, I can see the problem alright. What's the material? Looks like mercurium and gallirium?'

Me and Bossman tapped and poked and prised at this solid mouthful, 'They *are* teeth, aren't they?'

'I see what they mean about starving to death,' I said. 'You wouldn't get much oil-shale rock past that mass, would you?'

'Wouldn't do much chewing, either.'

'This stuff is a different mix from ours at the mine. It's titanium galloxide.'

I tapped and prised at a section. Then sledged and chackered at it, just to break a sample off. No effect. 'You know, Bossman, I believe it is. Awesome stuff.'

*

'So that's a no go,' we decided after a half-shift's labour with the chacker; then a line of blast caps; and a selection of diamond-tip, rotary and vibro drill bits.

'Definitely a new alloy. Could be valuable. Must be forty or fifty percent more resistant than the stuff we're digging out at Hades. And we're supposed to do this in a single shift? We've scarcely cleared around a single tooth.'

'Might be a *long* shift,' Bossman conceded, sort of smiling weakly while we walked round the head part, peering among the masses of white, grey and darker crystals.

'Yep, it could be a whole line of teeth protruding here and there,' I poked and pointed inside. 'And the idea is that we clear the whole lot out, so it can get back to eating and suchlike?'

'That's it.'

*

I connected up the Heavy-Four vibro bit, set it on three-quarter power, and hefted the tip at a convenient point in the crystal growth mass.

Another twenty mins; turning the power up; changing the bit; resetting the torque and vibration rates... got me precisely one fraction more than zero.

'Triple wages don't mean anything,' I told Sydun. 'Shifts don't last that long, even on Halcya. It'd have to be triple rate *per hour.*'

'You're not against giving it a try in principle, though?'

'Well,' I stood back and studied it. Massive great thing – an actual creature, this was. It turned a bit, angled down slightly. An eye broke open about crane-height above me. Staring at me. Yipps. 'It'll take some doing. Twenty or thirty days; maybe more. Hard work, especially if it was just me. Or both of us?'

He shook his head. 'Sorry. You're on your own for this job.'

I looked at the Heavy-Four diamond rotary vibro-drill bit I'd been using, its points dulled already.

'We're gonna need a bigger bit.'

WARPHANS

I must do more. After all the sacrifices that I and others have made, I cannot break faith with myself and give up now. Since losing my Donn four deccas ago, I realised I need somebody to look after. I have to keep doing my bit; help where I can.

There has been an appeal on the VT for homes for war orphans.

So I went to the emergency centre where they are housed; newly brought in from the conflict regions, wherever the fighting rages now. 'I'll do anything to help,' I said.

'Through here.' There was little time to consider, question or give answers and preferences. I wasn't fussy.

Looking into the room where they took me, I saw around twenty of them, all sizes and ages – playing or sitting around, chattering together, or rocking silently.

'What the Sholl is this?' I stared at the curling crustal shells, the triple tentacles, multiple fringe-fingers and blue-edged pincers. 'They're Kyohs, enemy kids; the things we're fighting in this war.'

'They're still kids. Same as ours... sort of—'

'They got flexilegs and arms! and eight fingers twice the length o' mine! Eyes like papercuts!'

'You really want to help, to make a difference? Here's your chance.'

I looked again. They were appalling excuses for life of any kind. I couldn't. Not possibly. Not those things.

*

One of the staff came home with me, on the pretence of checking my facilities, and staying overnight with me. But it was obviously mostly the scuff'n'coff she was interested in. Despite the war, I had a good supply, and we shared a second cup each. 'For a third cup in the morning, you can have three children,' she jested.

'Fairy Nuff,' I said. 'Do you have a User Guide? Starter Pack? Trial Period?'

'Yes. Yes. No – unless you get desperate and want to screw up the war effort.'

So three it was – two girl-equivalents called H'roke and W'hriss. Both injured somewhat, so I called them Broke and Twist – being, I was told, nine and six years of age. Human years? Must be about the same, I decided, with a lack of info on the subject from anywhere or anyone.

Then there was H'yenny. Tiny little jewel of a supposed male – though what the external difference was, I had no idea. My two new young ladies doted on him from the off – though none had known each other before.

I did a crash course – yes, I know, it was more of a four-night memo-drop on the language – but I spoke with them in Humanic – Standard Stang. 'You can learn as well,' I told them, 'if you're with me for any time.'

So weird. I didn't automatically like them. There was nothing about them to be likeable. We were all so wary of each other, keeping a few eyes open for the way out, I suspect.

I think the breaker was the third night when I heard a screaky sound from their room.

They were crying and cuddling together, and I stayed with them, laid on a fluff and raffia mattress they're supposed to like. I didn't dare move, and missed Part Two of the language drop. Level Two.

Next night, they came with me to my bed, skittering as though nervously. I didn't totally want to encourage them – I mean – they're angular, hard, and fidgety. But such dearies over the way they'd eaten up when I insisted and showed them how. Godsabove – their food tastes like something out the engine sump.

The war caused all this, 'And it's not helping now,' I told them.

We were having huge problems with power and heating, and food of any kind – despite the guarantees of supplies for our opponents' children. They didn't materialise after the first two deccas. 'Chibber ibber dik dik,' I told them. 'It's starve or eat the same as me.'

'Kiri wiri zip sip,' they said – which I wasn't sure about. But they tried it – mash and pseudo fish-meat-mush. I mean – who's positive about that when it first confronts you? They ate it. The following dec they asked for it again. I wasn't sure if that was because they actually enjoyed it, or because the food in the meantime had been even less appealing.

The war news was increasingly ominous; we were losing on so many fronts. But it was strange: I'd started taking them out to the park, for fresh air, and I found a couple of other mums were doing the same with their own babies and toddlers – humans. The reactions to my brood, after the initial days of incomprehension and disbelief, became smiling, touching, wanting to know. People seemed to like them, understand the situation.

Frankly, I was flabbered; and so pleased that my fellows hadn't pelted us all.

I cried when I sat at home. It had been the same as when I used to take my Donn to the park.

Our setbacks in the war seemed to fade away over the summer season, and we had news of a minor victory towards Year-end. Always rumours of new weapons, tactics, heroes... Nothing happened, of course. But we thrived on the desperation for positive news.

We? Me and three other mums and a dad who had adopted Kyoh orphans the same, and we used to meet in the park and at each other's houses a couple of times a decca.

The kids get on well together – like most kids. Two more joined us, but Massette was moving off-plan, and had to give hers up. So I offered; and welcomed M'yuti to be a companion for H'yenny – same size. So my girls had a youngy each to take under their winglets.

*

It was hard going. Rations were short – but goodwill wasn't. Not in the cafes or the park, or along the roadway, or the playground where kids of all three species mixed like they'd been born and raised together.

Three species? Yes, the HiMatte were in it by then, as intermediaries. They were doing a bit of brokering, peace-keeping, evacuating, rescuing. Diplomatty folk, they are; a bit downy-feathery with seemingly dozens of legs and squeaky voices. Quite a few Hi-Matte families had semi-settled here and were basically on our side, but, as theoretical neutrals, they were the obvious ones to act as negotiators. I always suspected they only did their bit so they'd be appreciated in lots of economic ways when it was over.

*

I heard about a couple of breakthroughs, and, 'We're going to win.' Yes, right; course we are. If we were really on the upside, the Gaddleys wouldn't have suddenly arrived among us – the fourth in our species mix. More rumours claimed they had been invited in, probably more accepted as neutrals than the HiMatte. Glossy ebon-skins and coiling tails; teeth like a zipp-saw. But their presence was seen as a sign of a new phase of some kind.

There were only two adult Gaddleys that I saw, and they joined-in with our group like they were observing. At first. But they had three of what they said were children, and when they got mixed up in the play and chatter, they all seemed to forget that semi-spying stuff that was rumoured about them.

We had dressing-up days – painting up all shining black one day and talking funny. Then wearing extra-long fingers another day, and talking funnier like the HiMatte. Being like humans another day, with long-haired wigs on their heads and talking weird. The Gaddley times with tie-on tails were floor-wetting funny.

It wasn't easy, with the differences in language, culture, wants, understanding. But kids are adaptable and pretty open-minded on important things. The adults were carried along with them.

*

'They're brokering a peace.' The news was all speculation and rumour. But was verified as the truth within the decca.

'There are difficulties...'

'The HiMatte and Gaddleys are struggling to keep both sides in the negotiating circle. You humans and the Kyohs have so much hatred built up, neither side can let it lapse even for a period at the tables.'

*

'I'm from the Gaddley Forum; the talks.' Someone who called himself Goot came to me and said. 'My children come to your Oppimisryhmä, your Learning Group. They say you have balance.'

'Does that mean I'm fat?' My Gaddleese isn't too good.

'You are fair, and you understand. You *see.*'

'So?'

'We wish to invite you to the talks between the two sides, as a consultant observer, with an impartial point of view—'

'I am *not* impartial. My Donn... I can't help you, not in all conscience.' I couldn't carry on, not with H'roke and W'hriss by my side, and clutching pincers with H'yenny and M'yuti. All with eyes swivelling up to me. 'My Donn... would have wanted... I'm on the side of the future, the children.'

It was a bit deep for me. It took some time to sink into Goot, too. I think he was taking a few deep breaths, or the equivalent in spiracle-sucking, before he decided what he wished to convey, and said he thought that was exactly what they wanted.

I wondered, aloud, if I might take the group with me. For them all to see each other. They considered, ummed and oikled, and agreed.

*

We went to the talks at the Gaddley Forum, and observed from a side suite that had clear panels for one wall.

Bless them all – we had thirteen Kyoh children by then – so excited to see their own people. Clamouring and tapping, whistling and shirrupping as never before, almost aglow. It spread among the HiMatte and the Gaddleys: all agog and high-eighting.

Until – about the third thing on the agenda, came the question of prisoner exchange.

The Kyoh delegation was shocked to a shell. 'We have no prisoners. Surrendees? They are vaporised. Yes – captives cost money. Solar-zapping is free. We do not keep them.'

The talks collapsed for the rest of the day, amid great ill-feeling among the humans, and distress among the HiMatte and Gaddleys – their intelligence on the matter had totally failed them. But, diplomats to the cortal lobes, the Gaddleys managed to get them all back together the next day, and the humans conceded, 'We have some of *your* people…'

Shocked, the Kyoh demanded to know, 'Who? From where? We won't pay for them. No value to us. No. No. We do not want any back. No matter what genderic orientation, age, status, injury. We refuse to negotiate over them.'

'We're not trying to negotiate. We wish to repatriate them, so they may rejoin you. If we can agree a place to meet for the excha— for the handover.'

'We do not want them. No matter who—'

My children were hearing it all. Then seeing their own people discuss it among themselves, questioning how valuable youngsters might be as sources of information about enemy habits, mores, weapons, deployments...

'I feel no affection for these people,' said H'roke.

'And I no allegiance,' said W'hriss.

'We want to remain with you, Rakastettu äiti. They are not our people.'

They said a lot more, besides, and so did everyone else around the tables and the halls. But we had the final say, and we stayed together. So did all the other Refugee-Kyoh children

It was the beginning of the end, perhaps. There was no further Kyoh aggression after that. It's thought the HiMatte and the Gaddleys threatened to support our side, actively, as well as tacitly. They began to wilt back; to retreat from several outposts they'd taken. Both sides began to offer and accept traders and builders, entrepreneurs and even the first of the adventure travellers.

*

I was asked the other day, by a Gaddley in a silver all-one garment – which is some high-status indication, I gather, if I would consider a post with the peace commission.

'As what?' My suspicion knew no bounds.

He hedged a little – shuffled several dozen legs, 'An example; your whole group, and perhaps my own children with them. And Kleemai's children as well, from the HiMatte contingent. I understand they join with your group?'

Mmm, they did, although I hadn't known they were silver-drops – top-rankers.

'One thing,' he hesitated again. 'A gross intrusion, but we have secretly vised you and your group several times, in various situations, recorded visi and audios of many things you have done together.' He looked at me for confirmation that I wasn't about to explode. 'And have circulated extracts among the Kyohs, as well as among ourselves, showing what may be achieved with goodwill.'

*

I was so doubtful. We all were; but we talked, and slept on it.

We didn't go for the visit to Kyoh the Home Planet – though none of us had ever been there before. There was still so much hostility generally; and the children were afraid. So we said we'd keep one day each decca to talk with whoever they bring to us. We all hated that, sitting and waiting in case someone came to speak with us – it was usually our day to do special things, like the Otake Forest Park, the Water Sports Centre, or the shopping Pallade. It was too much to miss out on, and we all hated the pointless talk anyway.

So we stopped doing that. 'They don't come very often and don't know what to say or ask,' H'roke and W'hriss noddled in agreement.

*

They still visi us one day a decca – I don't know which day – and use it for whatever propaganda they want. We agreed to it, and don't think about it. Not much, anyway.

Things are getting better: we're a proper family now, as families should be, and managing well. Like we laughed the other day, we all bless that first day in 6'44 when we first laid eyes, feelers and pincers on each other, and neither side was much impressed with the other.

EFFO

'Justa what I need, eh?'

I driva my lorry... my camion, witha twenty-eighta thousand kilos of finest Italian chocolate. I gotta get to the factory alle otto – like eight o'clock, eh? And what happen? Crashino sull'Autostrada Uno. The M1 all stop. All traffico in corsio rapido.

'Rapido? Fasta lane? Ha! Lungo wait – I gon be late.'

Sitting here. Traffico no move. Getting all dark. And I getting so I *needa* pipì. So I get outa my cab and stand there and do pipì in middle of M1 in alla the traffic. Nobody see. Not much – is a getting dark, eh? So I okay.

I see him. Is a man lying there. Behind the barriera. I finish pipì and climb over.

'He's a dead,' I tell police when I call il numero emergenza.

They say, 'Wait there anda we come.'

Then they come and tell me, 'He not dead. And you move wagon now.'

So I do a gooda deed, eh? Finda man in middle of-a road.

The police wished to be informed when the patient regained consciousness, and it fell to me as the Junior on Duty to make the call. Not onerous, but yet another irritation on a busy shift.

'Hello, I'm Doctor Willett. Concerning our patient, Mr Gebra?

'Gebra? Oh yes,' a very formal voice answered. 'He's the one from the M1, found unconscious in the central reservation? About three weeks ago, was it? Yes, I recall, we ID'd him, didn't we?'

I could hear him slamming filing cabinet drawers and cursing at disordered files in the depths of Mayor St Police Station. 'Ah, yes.' He'd found something. 'Local teacher. Mr Gebra. Norwegian heritage, Albert Gebra. What about him? Pretty smashed up. Died, has he?'

'No,' I said, 'he regained consciousness this morning, Sergeant. But he hasn't been making much sense. He did receive a blow to the back of the head in the incident. Depressed fracture. That's probably the cause of his confusion. Yes, exactly, *concussion*.

'As far as we can ascertain from his rambling, he last remembers being in the Lord's Arms some months ago, and seeing two of his former students in the public bar. He seems to recall they came into the Manor Lounge to talk with him.'

I waited while Sergeant Mallory spoke with someone else about another matter. As though his time is more valuable than mine. But I am a patient person, and my patient isn't going anywhere, as I explained to the sergeant.

'Mr Gebra was ranting and tossing about as if he was in a panicking dream. So much so that he had to be restrained. Yes, quite delirious, saying things like, "Syreena; I'll ring," and some long maths formula. And some other strange names – Norwegian, I suppose. "God. It was so weird", he kept saying. "So real-seeming".

'Best if you give it another day before you come and speak with him, hmm, Sergeant?' *At least a day*, I thought when I put the phone down, *the amount of haloperidol it needed to calm him down.*

🍷 'I do like men in uniforms,' I told this police officer standing there all stone-faced even when I gave him my widest smile and tightest pout. 'Oh, well,' I gave up, 'if you're ever free, hmm? This about Effo, is it? Mr Gebra, yeah. Yeah, me and Suzie were in the Lord's, weren't we, Suze? That was back in July, after school broke up for the summer. And we saw him looking at us. He was always nice – sweet, really. I know he always fancied me. And me and Suzie used to make up to him, din' we? So when the others came in, us two went round the posh bar to talk with him, and he still fancied me, I could tell.'

'Not like he'd ever do anything, though,' Suzie joined in. 'We wasn't maths-superbright enough for him – Effo only *really* liked anybody who loved maths as much as he did.'

'And nobody did, of course.' I gave the officer the bright eyes again, but he was immune. Probably queer.

'Effo?' he asked me.

'F.O. Fucking Obsessed. He always was.'

'He thought we were under-serious girls with a mustn't-work-too-hard attitude.'

'He was about right there.' Suzie giggled, and of course, once she started, I was off, too.

'He once said I was Dimbo Bimbo. Could'a got him sacked for that.' I had to smile at what I'd said to push him to saying it. Well, I got to, an't I?

'Yeah, we got him a drink in the Lord's and asked what he was doing – like was he still doing his schoolwork in the pub, and got his notebook out, an't he?'

'Always scribbling formulae and equations and things on bits of paper – fucking obsessed, he is.'

'Yeah, he's Effo, alright. Knew more than Einstein, we reckoned. We would have called him that, sep there was another teacher called Einstein already – him in the Languages department.'

'And it was Mr Gebra who was missing, was he? Effo? Since that night? I mean, it was months ago. We're getting ready for Christmas now, aren't we, Suze?'

'He been missing all that time? Since then?'

The policeman was nodding and making notes on his little tablet.

'No, we didn't stay in the Lord's, not after that tall Asian-type woman came over—'

'Like Thai, she was. I been there and she was like one of them dancers, only taller. No, we an't seen her before. But she sort of came and sat with him and started smiling and muttering—'

'Like they were soulmates—'

'Probably talking in numbers, knowing him – like "Six oh four double five nine".'

'Ooo, you cheeky devil. I do love it when you talk sums.'

'So when she came, we all left and went down the Cobbler's Last.'

'And he disappeared that night?'

So of course, Suzie started giggling again and that started me off...

At breaktime in school, they were saying that Albert Gebra in Maths had been found. It turned out he was the man from the motorway, near

Junction 28. So I said I'd go round the hospital and visit him, seeing as we had some history.

I rang and they said I could visit anytime on that ward. So I did.

'Oh, you look rough, Albi.' I says to him. 'They said you'd been hit by something and thrown behind the barrier by the impact? Wonder you haven't got more bones broken.'

He was shaking his head, as if he was wondering who I was.

'You must remember me? We teach at the same school. High Cross Academy? You can't have forgotten all that? Not you? Effo the maths genius?' I stroked his hand: I was still really fond of him, and he used to be super in bed.

'You and me?' He looked vacant.

'We were an item once. Quite a few times, actually, but I'm the sort who needs to get a look in with my partner, not play tenth fiddle to a formula.'

'All I want to do is inspire youngsters with the magic and beauty of maths.'

'They aren't up to it, Albi. But they do think you're sweet for trying. They take the piss something rotten behind your back.'

'Not all of them.'

'Don't smile like that, Albi,' I warned him. 'I know you had an affair with Lorrie McTaverne.'

'Okay, yes. Her. Not until two years after she left the academy.' He had this sort-of winning little smile sometimes. And he did then.

'You don't know about the others, then?' he smiled again. 'Effo I may be, but some young ladies seem to think I need diversion and consolation of a more physical kind. They're very good at trying to distract me.'

'So you're a thirty-year old child prodigy sex maniac? Don't look so smug about it.'

'If some delightful young lady thinks she's the cure to my mathematical compulsion, and is fairly insistent about it, who am I to thwart her... *them?* Never once with a current student. Only ever when they'd moved on to higher things.'

He could be insufferably complacent sometimes.

'As the Police Community Liaison Officer, I have been detailed to speak with you before you are discharged, Sir. We have considered your record – or lack of it. Nothing criminal, unless we count finding yourself in here twice previously – victim of domestic violence on both occasions. Hmm?'

'Ex lady-friends who decided they couldn't stand being in bed with a calculator any longer.'

'But you didn't defend yourself in any way on either occasion? It's not as if you're a small person.'

He deep-sighed, all philosophical-like. 'I imagine they needed to vent something on me.'

'Three broken ribs on one occasion; broken arm on the other?' I quoted to him from my notes. 'Some venting.'

'They got over it. So did I. Do you know what happened to me this time? I remember some of my old students coming over to talk with me in the Lord's Arms. Someone bought me a drink. Did they drug me?'

'Not that we know. You went missing for four months, and you've been in here for the past four weeks, since you were found laid out in the central reservation on the M1. You'd been lying there, between the central barriers, for three days, six hours, and twenty minutes – until our HGV caller spotted you, and rang 999.'

'Oh? Such precision in the timing?'

'CCTV network for traffic control – there's a static camera situated thirty metres from where you were found. There's footage of you the whole time. It shows you appear – suddenly, from nowhere. Lane Three – the fast lane. Headlights on you; you stood there for around one second, and were hit from behind by a dark blue Ford Transit. Threw you sideways between the barriers, and you never moved again – three days. Might still have been there if it wasn't for the incident that shuffled the high-cab drivers into Lane Three.'

'And I simply appeared?'

'Out the blue – or black, it was four a.m. One second to the next. If there wasn't the terrorist alert on, they said they'd investigate further. But Special Squad were up to their necks in it – no-one to spare. "Aberrant camera fault" it's gone down as. The offending vehicle had been stolen. It was found burned-out in Leicester. Wonder you didn't freeze to death, unmoving for that length of time.'

Now then, was there anything else? I consulted my notepad. 'And you have no idea where you were the rest of the time? Seventeen weeks without a sighting, no use of a card. Your car didn't move an inch. You didn't go to your house – your neighbour noticed and rescued your cats. She reported you missing, twice. There was a *brief* investigation.'

'You didn't bother much, then?'

I shrugged and told him straight, 'You're adult, no dependents – no unidentified bodies turned up – you're free to vanish if you want. End of the school year, you could easily have decided to call it quits, new career, new ID. Get away from ex-lady friends, perhaps?'

'Right,' he looked at me, 'like I'd want a new mortgage; new women problems; and no job?'

'Well, whatever, Sir. Our involvement is ended.' I snapped my notebook off to let him know. 'We do not envisage any charges to be pending against you or anyone else.'

$F = G \dfrac{m_1 m_2}{r^2}$ They threw me out the hospital two days after that. 'We need the bed space. Your memory is returning. Here's a number for Social Services. Goodbye.'

'Thanks Doc, you've been good.' I went home. Didn't want to know about school, but I rang and they didn't want to know about me, either, as it was coming up to Christmas and end of term. They'd hired a replacement for me long ago. I'd have to re-apply to come back.

Four months? Dated from that night in the bar. When... Yes, Suzie and Dimbo Diane came over in the pub. She did buy me a drink, laughing about something. Me, probably. They went... and... and... Someone else was with me.

Young woman; very smart, fluid movement. It was like I saw the formula to quantify her movement as she sat with me. Almost a Far-Eastern face – the really, *really* smart kind. I just about fell in love there and then. If I could have made a poem up out of formulae, she'd have been it, in motion.

Actually, I think I did fall for her. She pushed a double Lagavulin and Fevertree my way, and when she started talking algorithms and vectors, I was hers. I remember drinking and talking, and my head spinning. She was captivating in her face and figure, her buying and drinking capacity, and her awesome ideas on conceptual mathematics. Even to me, the thinking was lateral – and lateral thinking's my five-tay – that's like a forte, but one up.

Jeeps, yes; she was opening little number boxes in my head. I was whirling inside. All so much. Nirvana for a Nerd, it was.

That's when it all goes dizzy and mixed up in my head.

I went with her, I'm sure. Far end of the back car park, behind the skittle alley. It was the absolutely typical sci-fi blue light. Perhaps more UV, actually. Beam me up, Scottie.

After that... *Shyze!* It's building up, what I remember. The faces, and what they were saying, asking. They were all so fantastic-looking. And the maths!!! I was in this like ultra-mod space-shuttle-type control room. And everyone was talking in maths. And asking me as though I knew it all, too. I didn't at first, but I was getting the hang of it – and I was learning in leaps and frogs. It went on for ages and ages... like day after day in this super-sci-fi-spaceship-type place. Weeks.

It keeps coming back to me in fragments. It wasn't supposed to be like this. I don't think I planned for a Ford Transit, plus three days down the middle of the M1 and a month in hospital. No. I was supposed to do something.

The maths, yes... Three-dimensional navigation algorithms. Representational vectors. And speeds! They were talking, no, not talking, *thinking* at me, in Plus-light mechanics; supra-physics. I don't know if there's a name for it – some way-out branch of astro-physics to do with non-finite Euclidean space.

Yesss... I was there. Somewhere. Their equipment had failed. They didn't have the skills. The concepts, yes, but not what to do with them – a whole clicking and clucking navigation system for a spaceship.

It was ridiculous. I'd been on a spaceship, working out how to navigate it without the electrono system they usually relied on. Got themselves stranded somewhere hereabouts.

I'd travelled – been moving in it – stars round us – blurring, changing colour, huge red-shift. Plus-light, they called it. By trial and error, I think, we went to two planets that we were actually looking for. Not in one go, but we worked it out in stages, set up a mytronic system, and got the next two right. Spot on.

Godalone knows where they were – or are. I mean, I know how to get to them, but *where* they are is anyone's guess. Somewhere in the mathematical nexus. And it was me who'd found the way – they knew the branch, but I'd found the way.

And sex! Yes, I do remember that – three were women. Utterly dreamtime fantasy gorgeous. Hellfire, yes, I recall the sex.

I also recall glimpses of them looking distinctly non-human – not like they're a cross between a crayfish and a squid, but not quite entirely *human*, either. However, back to recalling the sex, they were plenty near enough to being a very attractive form of lady.

And that was it. Was it? I was going to... what? Resume my life? So-called life. No, that can't have been it.

☎ I'm spending so long trying to remember. They dropped me off so I could... something. Before returning to them, to join their crew. Forever. Well, permanently, anyway. Forever is a concept that— never mind right now.

But the drop-off must have gone slightly awry: location a touch wrong. Middle of the M-bloody-1. I was back to straighten things up – Millie and Colin, the cats. The bank, my house. Job. Sort them out. Clear up all my affairs here – *financial* affairs, that's all. Then take off with them again when I was done, Heading for space unknown. Or I would know, actually – as the new navigator.

Yes, that was it. The job – the most fantastic life. I never even dreamed of anything so perfect. I only need to contact them, and I'll be on an ultra-light-speed spaceship, talking maths, with a group of the most amazingly wondrous alien females in existence.

Now, if only I could remember the number I'm supposed to ring to arrange the pickup...

THEY'RE ONLY HUMANS

'If we manoeuvre straight in, Number Two, we'll still be on schedule. So get in there, *now*. Stop patty-footing round, and do it. On time.' We must be on time. All these delays are intolerable. We're one of the biggest freightliners in the whole sector – Two thousand passengers and forty-two cargo holds. *We're big.* Too big to be kept waiting. Especially when we're part of an all-sector company like Heritek Trading, Passenger and Mining Incorporated.

'By the chocks of Kohri! We're going in much too slowly.' I watched our progress on the counters and screens. We'll be in a berth half a yeck beyond schedule at this rate, and that will cost me. 'Number Two, get us in there *now.*'

'Not possible, Captain. We need to keep below eighteen mpf within the port control area.'

'And wait for Control permission to approach and be allocated a berth... and docking number,' Sub Yains was sticking his proboscis in. 'There'll be other ships in line as well. It's a busy port – I mean, just look at it.'

'I don't need to look at it – a tangle of girders and cranes; lights and total shadows. They're all the same, from one vidshow to the next telecom. So get us in, now.'

'Port Control said to wait, to halt at the out-marker. They have other vessels—'

'Just get out the way, Two. I'll do it myself.' I pushed him aside; it's not as if I was new to the game – eleven years as Number Two on other vessels. And we all kept our skill-set well-tuned. You can do so much more with these modern craft than you could even twenty years ago. 'Tell Engines to patch power through to my console. Send off a word to Port Control informing them that we need to be in now. Then cut the communication channel.' I must hurry. Or, cursit, I'll lose my Punctuality Bonus, and earn a blue mark on my trip record.

Right. I know I look good standing at the control console – we have passengers in sometimes, and that's when I adopt the heroic stance they love. 'I'll take the nearest berth to the entry point. There, yes; that one looks fine. See? The grapples are already moving back in auto-mode to accommodate something of our size.' Speed's a bit high, but I have the fore-burners, and can trip the main engine into reverse – just a blip is usually sufficient. Simple. Going so well.

Darrit! There's some shitty little ship tucked in, over in the far corner of the berth. Hadn't seen him. Ah well, he'll have to move. I'm not stopping this mill-tonner for the sake of some local tramp trader.

Ha. It's not even a Federation vessel. So it's of no consequence. 'Shut the bloody comms off.' I was sick of Control's attempts to break back in, telling me to halt, back off. No chance. Wrong berth? Me? No such thing when you're my size.

Permission? Just you try *not* giving permission – against a mill-tonner from Heritek Inc.

So I'm going in. That turdy little craft is some humanic heap. That's the HumRaD logo all over it. Huh – like they're something. They are – pack of sheff hounds sniffing round for scraps and dodgy business. Easy enough to nudge aside; make room for us.

Humanic Realm and Dependencies? Huh. 'Come on, squidgy one, out the way.'

'That Humanic pilot's panicking,' Senior Port Control Officer Otle was furious. 'He's yelling at us. Like we've got time to listen to him when there's a mill-tonner coming in and paying no attention to regs and permission. The captain of the Pride of Heritek's taken direct control of the whole entry procedure – what the yoik does he think he's doing? That's not permitted at all. He's not qualified for port entry. Certainly not this port. Yoikit – You deal with the HumRaD pilot, Zimi. I'll try to manage the Pride.'

'I'll see if I can placate the human pilot, Sir. He's definitely going to be hit, though. And that won't look good on our records.' Zimi winced in anticipation of the impending crunch.

'The Pride's got a registered port officer in there, along with his regular Nav and Second, but he's not letting any of them give active support.'

'Oh, Yoiks! He is… he's going to impact the HumRaD vessel – the Mary Starr. Slow, but it's a collision just the same.' Zimi's frills were full-erect, eye stalks popping.

'And therefore obligatory to report. Shuggit – more backtime filler work to irritate me.'

'Gaff! Gaff! He's hitting now. Oh, no; look at that crumpling. That little'un's suffering. Shoiks to Dodds! He'll be lucky to surv—'

'Get that liner captain on the TriVee now. This is criminal. He's in for the Hijo.'

'Heed now. This is the final judgement on this matter.

'Captain Egoista of the Mill-tonner Pride of Heritek is held to be Not at Blame. The incident was at the fault of the captain of the small Humanic craft, the Mary Starr, which had taken unauthorised entry to Berth F2. Control failed to maintain complete oversight of either vessel, and is judged to have been negligent in maintaining proper order in the port at the time.'

SPC Officer Gaff Otle listened impassively to the judgement as it was made public. He had made his representations earlier, and was now bound to follow Authority rulings, like them or not.

'In a gesture of goodwill, however, Heritek Incorporated, owners of the Pride of Heritek, have agreed to pay a sum in the amount of three hundred thousand Yu to the Port Control Authority in compensation for the inconvenience. That is the end of the matter.'

'What?' Standing beside Otle, Zimi drooped a mandib in disbelief. 'What about the Mary Starr; the little HumRaD craft? It was there first. I gave it permission... allocated it there.'

'No, you didn't. Study the records. It pushed in. Shouldn't have been there.'

'Yes, Sir. It—'

'You want to keep your job, Zimi? Yes? Therefore, you *didn't* give permission. Take the payout and shut up. That other craft was only a Humanic – slithery things, like giant slurghs. Hardly important, are they? Three of four HumRad vessels have been doing petty trading around the region for the past year or so. Not exactly significant on a spiral scale, are they? Include them in discussions? Compensation? What for? They're only humans.'

'Sir, it's not right. He had permission. He's been in, protesting his perspective; his loss. He wants repayment for the severe damage and loss of cargo. It was the freightliner—'

'The mill-tonner? Owned and run by the biggest corporation in the region? More vessel-tonnage; more passengers; more income from them than any three other companies. We do *not* find against them. Ever. One more word, Zimi, and you're out of work, and I'll ban the humanics from docking here again, anywhere in the port. This is a *Krabba* orbital station, not HumRaD. They got no rights here.'

Zimi wasn't intending to let it rest without a full protest. 'It came to plead its case, again, you know, the humanic? Came to me in person—'

'And you sent him to me. Yes, thank you for that. "I've been coming here for best part of a year," it tried telling me, as if that gave it rights. "Three of my fellow humanics, too. We're hoping to build up our involvement here; could be more of us coming later; increase trade hereabouts. Benefit everyone."

"'Not going to happen, Humo," I told it. "We judge after the initial period of new contacts; and set your status. Yours is now set at second level, so use the side port in future – and you shouldn'a been there if a biggy's heading in." Course, it's all protest and hands-out for supposed compensation, but it didn't help it.

'I warned him, "Shut up. Go away now. Or you're barred for good." Damned squidgies – time they had decent morphology and metabolism, not that repulsive soft, flexi shape. It's what comes of eating all that stinking gunge they always want. Yeuky creatures.'

Zimi was getting the picture, and knew he was on a loser if he carried on protesting. 'Right, Sir; not another word from me, but I've watched 'em, and I think there's more to 'em than squidge and gunge. But,' he hastened, 'I had my say to you, and the Board, and the two humans I spoke to—'

'Zimi,' Otle warned, flicking a chito in his subordinate's direction, and vibing his middle eye cluster towards the exit. 'You'll be out on your carapsids if I hear of this again.'

Zimi was gone, clicking his pinzetti in frustration.

We took it. Not much choice, of course. Port Traffic Control and the Governing Board had spoken. As expected, they favoured their own multi-planet corporations over any concept of justice.

Most of them, it's grab-and-stuff for yourself. Take advantage wherever you can. Like most folk back home, I guess. Except an occasional one here and there.

'Come on, Kissa. Time we radded back to Base.' A scratching tickle under my companion's chin elicited a purr of agreement. 'We're coming up to the full year's assessment time, anyway. Got to report soon. Might as well get it done now.'

So I sat with Kissa on my lap, waiting while she tuned the connection in. Then stabilised it and verified identities at each end. She was so good at it, 'Beautifully done, Kissa. I really wanted to give them every chance. Ahh, well done. Here we are, through to Base.'

'Okay, Neko-ko, give us the details again.' Base Officer Wiren wanted a full run-down on the year's key experiences as well as this latest incident. 'Yes, I know you have, but I want to hear it all again.'

So I had to go through the whole year's highpoints and turning points...

'Okay,' he eventually concluded, 'we assess them after the initial period; I reckon we've had enough time now. Plenty of evidence to judge from.'

'It all seemed reasonable – even positive – on the first impressions we had,' I tried to re-make the case for them. 'I thought it was possible to work with them, cooperate. Then they come up with that, what the port controller told me, "Listen, Yeuk. You're here on sufferance. Repulsive creatures like you will never make it here. You don't get rights, and you don't get docking space."'

'Yes, yes,' Base Officer Wiren sighed, 'if they still haven't even begun to measure up with the equal rights, access and cooperation option, then I'm afraid it's Option 2 – Domination. Okay, Neko-ko?'

I sighed, resigned to it. It was what I'd expected. I stroked Kissa's silken fur as B.O Wiren summed up with the inevitable.

'I'll get on to High C Space Command. I'll see when they can find time to fit in a quick Invade, Occupy and Dominate Action. Yes, thankyou— Dammit, Neko-ko, you finished reporting. The Krabbas had the chance. It's what they do with the little guys that measures their worth – just needs the right trigger to tell.'

'But they're not too—'

'You're finished on this one Neko-ko. *We* take over. You're off.'

'But—'

'*You're done, Otoko.* Your role is to observe and report. At most you can recommend – and we've listened to you and heeded your view. So no more. You've earned a break now. Finished a luna earlier than expected, huh? So use the time – have yourself a rest, spend some time relaxing with your family.'

I watched the screen fade and blank to a pink point. 'You hear that, Kissa? We're going to annexe the Krabba Federation.' My lap companion purred, and nuzzled my hand. 'Me? Base wants me to have a rest. A rest? Twenty-eight extra days with *my* wife? They think that's a rest? I don't expect her mood and attitude will have improved a lot just lately. A full luna in her company, with nothing to be occupying me? That'll be wonderful, won't it?'

Kissa purred in her ever-gorgeous way, nudging my hand for more head-scratching.

'I wonder: if I ask Wiren really nicely, might Base send me the details for my next assignment immediately, so I can start working on my approach strategy? And maybe arrange an urgent call bringing the timing forward?

'Anything but an extra luna with Misrabelle.'

SOMETHING TO BE DONE

I'm no Lookout. I was busy drilling outside the camp compound – just exploratory surveying on my own, prospecting for any more platinum-group ores outside the main mining area. Not supposed to be any risk on whichever rockball this is.

No sound in the vac to warn me.

A red flare lit everything up. Things lashing past me. Huge explosion. I'm turning. The whole camp erupting in one supra-blast. Not so much as a blip or a squawk on anything electronic. Completely caught-out and wiped-out we were. *Shike! That's the end of our mining this asteroid.*

Ten, fifteen seconds later, I'm still watching the huge red fireball swell away from the surface and up into the Big Black. *Damn Astons have found us.*

'Mop-up crew next,' I'm saying to the laser as I get the power switched up.

Sure enough. Five more seconds, and I saw this GH fighter swinging in. Almost too late spotting him, spiraling down out the black sky, silver-black lobster-craft, bristled-up with weaponry, dropping towards our ex-camp – just glowing red-black rubble now. Fast little scuffer, expecting to scorch survivors out. He'll be lucky; bet there ain't none left, 'cept me out here on the rim.

'Come on, come on… I'm powered up and ready, you evil little scuffer.' Famous last stand on Astro 4-0-4 this was not going to be. Infamous, maybe. Last, definitely. 'Come on. You're just one last something to be done.'

So I'm waiting. I've got to be the only survivor on the surface, tucked out here with my prospecting hog. It was obviously going to be the Astons who'd done it, and this was the first one coming in now. *Death itch duly scratched. 'Come on... come on...'*

Swung my laser artic round. It's as good against ships as it is against solid rock that needs segmenting. 'Come on, just get in range, you little scuffer.' Shikit. Another behind it. And Mr Biggy coming overhead. It'll have a dozen GHs nestling in and around it. They always do. How the scuff had they snuck so tight? Managed to get close enough to fire without any spitback from us? Where the Shike was Freddie the Watch? He's the one who's supposed to be Lookout, not the rest of us guys.

Another, out of range but homing fast. I can take the small closer one. Probably the next as well. But not enough time to recharge before the others have me spotted. I'm a damn miner now-days. Not a guardsman – gave that up years ago.

Koh, so I homed in on the first one, knowing it'd be the next to last thing I did. *Power's up, Aston. You're mine.*

Nicely in close. *Come on... in a bit more.* Not aware of me, nestling here among rocks. Yes, he's centred beautifully. Easing on the button... 'You're dead,' I whispered, thumb holding place. 'Take a few of you with me. Any sec now. Wait. Nearly ripe for it...'

Like I want any of them for company on my Last Orbit?' My thumb didn't go down. It just stayed there, settled, not pressing.

'What's the scuffing point?' *We oughtn't to be here. None of us should be. Scruggit, I'm done for, whatever I do. Bit of a shame it's like this. But it's well overdue.* I let my thumb slide off the button. 'We asked for it, I guess.' I'd take it, quick, like the others had. *It's my turn. An instant and I'll be gone. Yeah, about time, considering the last few jobs I've had. Didn't expect to last this long. Just unlucky, I guess.*

Watched my power readings collapse. My power halo would have faded outside. No point. I watched on the screen. The incomer wasn't even powered on – no rating showing. *I can still take the stupid little toe-rack.* Then Mr Biggy cruiser'll get me in four... three... two... one. *Come on. Come on. Fry me. Please.*

Nothing. I was staring up at them. Huge ship hovering half a squidge overhead. I'm waiting for the bloom, a nano-sec before I vap out of existence. Nothing.

Two little GHs come circling over me. Vibrating red and blue halos round their weaponry ports. *You should have fired.* 'Come on. Get it over.' *Being a prisoner'd be worse than being dead.*

But they didn't. GHs might be small as spacecraft go, but they're ten times my size – groundhog driller. They closed, dropped electron grapples on me. *Shikit, No. The Astons don't treat captives well. Damn. I should'a let loose at the reckless little scuffer in the van. Too late now – I'm de-powered.*

**

It was a dark time – hoisted into their cargo ship. Packed with gunnery, but it wasn't the cruiser I thought it was. Dull grey satin walls and beams closing all round me in the hold. Dim lighting. A voice in really awful broken Fed-speak ordered me out.

So out I climbed, into a huge transport bay with two of their GHs lined up. Never seen one close before. Near as big as our Miner had been. *Scruggit, we're tiny, compared with their operation.* A welcoming group of three of them – adult Astons, with the triple sets of antennae.

They grilled me for around ten minutes. Mostly, they seemed to be evaluating me for threat level, and decided I was a Zero – beat-up heap like me.

Then they quizzed me on my skill as an operator of the mining rig. I was in two minds about showing them how it operated, but I'd heard tales of how they treat prisoners: they don't believe in rights. You're a slave with only work-value. No point stirring their paddles – they'd get rid of me when they knew how to operate the blasting sequencers and melters. *Like I got a choice? They don't kill nicely, so I've heard.*

Except they didn't get rid of me. I was dumped in a rusted iron bay with some Rhoy types – the green-tinge, sluggy eyes, and girdle frills lot. It seemed they'd been captured some time back, and expected to be used as miners on some high-risk roid.

Apart from the Rhoy, a gang of Krill took up most space, and they were noisy, belligerent and bent on trouble. How they were ever taken prisoner, I've no idea. I crawled down the other end of the bay, *Keep out their way, Lanni*, I'm telling myself. They were scrugging about with something – one of the other prisoners. I caught a flash of old-gold-on-midnight – Corp Officer. Scrugg, a Terran – humanoid, anyway. I got no love for the military wings, none whatsoever. But species stick together. That's Absolute. You don't, ever, leave your own in the hands of another type. Or in their feelers, in the case of Krill.

So I pushed through. Lot of raised eye-slots at me, daring to do that. But I worked with Krill on Jackson Four and know their little ways.

Yeah, it was someone in Corp uniform they'd got. I reached and grabbed the collar. Lifted. 'Up you come. You're with me. Been looking for you.' Stared round them all. 'This one's *mine*. Any object?' You put it in that tone and mode, and they know you're serious. I guess they weren't that bothered. They wanted bother with the Astons, not humans.

So I dragged him away, 'Keep your head down. Be humble; subservient. They need to think we're master and slave.'

But he was struggling and cussing like a regular. 'Let me go! I'm an effing officer! How dare you.'

'Shykit. You're a *she*. And an officer. In the Corp. I usually limit myself to two clangs per day.'

We ate the stang paste that everybody and everything got in space. The Rhoy lot loved it, even though it curled their frills. I was nearly vomiting on it, but forced it down; power-packed for nutrition and survival. She ate it and said nothing more till she'd finished. Then told me she was Trainee Orlea, Captain of a Seek Destroyer. Not that *Captain* meant a lot. 'I was training to manage a pack of recruits, so the captain rank is honorary. We were waylaid in an unarmed buggy, practising landing on some dungheap out in the Alvin Cluster. And that's clearly ours; not in dispute.' She spat a lump of something unwelcome out the Stang paste, 'I think the others were wiped-up. I was taken.'

But she didn't know much about the Krill and the others. Was scared of them. Knew she'd been for the chop and drop with the Krill. Also, she hated underlifers and dungarees. And I was both, in Aces.

We were never going to get on, me and Captain Orlea. I hate the Corp; loathe officers; and despair over women. I got nothing against women per se – not lately, anyway, so I suggested she got rid of the officer colours. 'There's spare dungs in my module. You'll not be so conspicuous.'

Fruggs to Mary! You'd think I just raped her over a jack-hammer rig.

'Do it or don't,' I told her. 'But you'll attract less attention in drags same as mine.'

So she did. Ill of grace. And we dossed down not exactly together, but pretty close. Enough to be seen as together. Therefore less vul.

Four days like that. Like slop-pigs in the bilges. But alive, just about. *Big deal, but maybe best not to be too reckless now she's with me. Yes, of course she's with me. Species stick together. Be told.*

We must have arrived somewhere. The usual three Astons came in, barking about, 'Get in your mecho units.' Half a period later we were being shuffled out and dropped onto a rocky surface – airless. The instructions were to survey an area eighty kay across, and map out the lodes of spirithium, plus anything else that registered above nine-five on the nanos. That was straightforward enough. The Krill didn't think so. Cost two of them their lives – dismembered screaming and whistling. So the others cottoned on and cooperated after that.

Me and Orlea, they just made us work, kept watch and mostly ignored. An occasional electro-bolt to wake us up, or speed us up.

They killed one of the Rhoy – sliced him in a grinder. Seems he'd been polluting the samples. Deliberate sabotage, they evidently took seriously. We all missed the stang slop that day. They were simply uncaring about their prisoners; we were nothing to them. Just work units to be used up. Orlea didn't help a lot: she had a stroppy streak and would have let it answer back sometimes. So I clouted her and forced her down on her knees. It kept her alive, but it sure stoked up her loathing for me.

It was a bad attack of the silverdust mites that laid me out. The Astons were gonna ex me, but something stopped'em. They must have known what it was, and knew I'd recover. Not wanting to waste a good working unit. Besides, to protect her, I'd showed Orlea how to operate the rig by then, and she reckoned that was why I survived.

'So you should be on your knees in gratitude,' she told me. I wasn't too sure how she figured that.

The supervisors didn't come outside to fetch us back in one day, on some light-gravity planet we'd been moved to. 'Been some sort of trouble?' we were debating. Lot of restlessness about what might happen with us, but we all re-assembled close to the ship, anyway, although some wanted to escape when the dark was spreading in.

'Y' mad? Where else is there to go?' I said. 'I know how the ramps and doors work, and the stang spigots. Extra rations for anybody who feels the need.'

They were all highly dubious, especially Orlea – all Officer and Attitude. 'You must be a spy for the Astons if you know things like that 'So how d'you know?

'I use my eyes, Your Officership.' *Where do they get'em these days? Half the rank I had, and enough snot for the whole brigade.* 'Shikit, Orlea, we *need* to be inside overnight, whatever bother the Astons are having.'

I worked the ramps and doors and spigots, and we survived the night, same as always, pigged out across the bay in our own little communities, 'cept we fed ourselves when we wanted, all night.

Astons looked at us next morning. Said nothing. They had new prisoners: Co-Man spacers. Semi-humanoid, but they had a stench to their mentality as well as body. In five clicks and a whistle, you could tell they weren't very accepting of being prisoners – trying to stir the rest of us up to rebellion. Some of the Krill were up for it.

'Don't get tempted,' I told Orlea.

'It's our duty—'

'Your duty is to stay alive and learn. It's the Astons who're top nail here. We might be their prisoners, but we need to stick with them. The Co-Mans are as bad as the Astons, and the Krill are just up for anything riotous. They'd all eject us if they had chance. Now get in the module and we'll be powered up and waiting to start work when they come for us.'

'Traitor.'

'Me? Am I scrugg. I'm totally loyal to what's best for me. And you. So have some sense.'

We exited as usual when the ramps went sliding out, raking and scooping, drilling and searing, setting the various melts and collecting containers. Most of the Rhoy and the Krill came with us in their rigs, and started up as usual.

Orlea was sulking all day. 'You're the biggest coward and collaborator the universe's ever known. 'I'll see you're Corp-marshalled if we ever escape from here.'

'Shuffle-off, Off. The Corp tried that before. It din't work. They got no hold on me any longer.'

They let us back in the transport hold as the red little sun slid away. The others' modules were there, but the rebellious remainers weren't. All the new Co-Man group were missing, along with the Krill who'd refused to go out.

Bit of a recrimination mood around the bay that off-shift. Everyone – Orlea leading – was unsure if I should be blamed for not backing the rebels; or credited with not getting us killed alongside them. The balance seemed to be that everything was my fault. *Right. Whatever.*

It was a cold night. Me and Orlea had never been near doing anything intimate, anyway, but she was more distant than usual that night. 'I don't much care what any of you thinks,' I told her. 'We're alive, and half the others aren't.' So I rolled over, self-justifying, cold, fake-powered by the stang, detested by the only other human there, still silverdust-weak, and with a left arm that was getting the flesh-rot. But still alive. That was a bit of a nuisance. Almost disappointing.

'No point throwing y'life away, your Officerdom,' I told her. 'Save it for something worthwhile. It's what I'm doing.'

You would not believe the look she gave me. I could see her verdict lighting her up already: "To be Airlocked". Typical officer. Total belief in the corp creed

'It occurs to me, Orlea, Captain, Sir-Mam, that Co-Mans don't go round in little packs, like the few they captured and threw in here. So where are the others? They have the herd instinct in gold. There'll be more of them. And they'll not be happy little bugs.'

Now. If I can wonder if there's some further trouble in the offing with the Co-Mans, then surely the Astons could. But they didn't have out-lookers posted around our works area, so we'd have to do it ourselves. 'You're on lookout today,' I told Orlea. 'Nothing else. I'll do all the S and T work.'

'Why?'

'Co-Mans are swarm-oriented. They're nasty little scuffers, and they'll be worse than usual when they know their oppos have been wiped away. Stay full-peeled. Especially for anything coming out the glare of the sun. You see anything move in the shadows. You scream and you press that.'

'What's that do?'

'Boosts the laser – all power gets diverted there. Scream loud enough so I hear. Koh? Relying on you. I'll be out the module and getting on with the probing, or the Astons'll zap us if they're suspicious.'

The survey and testing was good that day. Pleasingly productive on a known streak, and I found a new one leading off. We followed it through and logged a big vug of crystal varanite. They'd got to be chuffed about a find like that – but you don't tell the turd it done good, do you? So none of the Astons said anything.

No sign of Co-Mans all day. Orlea was pissed. Bored. But I was i/c. So she did it next day as well. And the next; furious with me. And I didn't waver. I was damn sure the Co-Mans would come back – some would have escaped. And would be back in force.

Out the setting sun they came, low and fast, between and over the rock peaks. Orlea – may the Pit bless her – was still attentive. 'It's that or no supper,' I'd told her. Her scream jumped me out my suit. But I was tuned for it – one second and I was spun, thumbing the trigs and looking. *There.* Three I saw on the inst. And zapped the direct-heading-for-me one – little light-panel attacker. Locked in on him and he was puff. The other two, both off to my left, veered round, manoeuvring for positional attack on the base mod. I cut them both out – *six years in Corp Gunnery not wasted after all.* And vapped a fourth homing in on me.

That was me finished – banks wouldn't re-power for at least a minin. 'Till then, we sit and pray, Orl.'

We took a glancing pow from something, but I had the screens re-starting by then, and it only took out the fuse banks.

Saw others, more distant. Zipping round, getting themselves vapped.

We were out there all night. Orlea was her usual self, 'So the Astons still have us? Proud of yourself, are you, Dunger?'

'Still not a happy little officer, Orlea?'

Pits – it was black – a few stars. Not many. No food. Power low. Freezing by dawn. They came for us a quarter after sunrise. Astons, of course.

They ordered us to work. Zapped us in temper.

I buzzed, 'We need power.'

One of them must have cottoned on, checked our bottoming levels. We got ordered in, then grappled in when our power faded completely.

It was rough. Damn Astons didn't want to know anything, just to screw us round for losing power. And they dragged us out the module. I got worked over. Scrugg, the Astons know how to hurt. I burned and screamed everywhere. Didn't know if it was punishment or they wanted to know something. They were on a loser, either way.

I could imagine what they were doing with Orlea; much the same, I suspected. I tried to ask. Received a pincer across my face for my trouble. Broke my nose, by the feel of it. Dragged me off. Interrogated me. Didn't understand much of the Aston-Fed-Standard mix language they were using, and I wasn't all attention, anyway. Wanting to know about Captain Orlea. *Why the shufty do I care about her? She hates me. Yeah, but she's human. Sort-of.*

They got serious. Had me down on a pale blue meditable somewhere inside the main body of the ship. I was stripped off naked. Not nice. While they examined me like they'd never got to grips with a human before. A smarter trio of Astons this time.

Needles probed inside me. Inserting things, removing bits. Scrugging painful. I tried not to screech too much. But I'm never too successful at hiding agony. I kept telling them about pain – but I think the concept was beyond them.

They faded away – in reality or in mind, I dunno. But they came circling back with electro machinery – drills, cutters, saws, slicers... Needles. Hovering over me. Something in my throat. Deep. *Checking for the silverdust,* I thought. Them and the machines making whirry sounds, one holding a circular cutter that came down at my arm and went straight in at my elbow.

I shrieked and jerked away – stump for an arm. My elbow gashed wide open. *They're dissecting me.* Nothing to lose then by resisting, so I let'em have it. Pushing and thumping against the restraints and trying to get up and kicking, and they were all over me, carapaces flapping, tendrils lashing out, some penetrating me. And I was secured at all points by tendrils and tentacles and murmuring clickles and beeps.

They had the cutter back, and I couldn't move a muscle. Not even to scream when the spinning little thing came back into me, turning and twisting and slicing in—

Hadn't dismembered me. My left arm, the fleshrot part below the elbow, was gone. They were fiddling and smearing, stopping the blood. Didn't act like they knew about blood.

Got me up. I'm shaking and collapsing, and they started telling me something, like I should be over it by then. But they were talking only in Aston, and I never let on that I understand more than a few words. It makes it easier to listen in sometimes.

Two of them were new seniors, but they knew my name. One was chirruping that I didn't fire at their incoming craft right at the start. And hadn't joined the rebellion. 'You are Lannister. Former FSN Officer Lannister. You took out the first wave of Co-Mans yesterday?' He was highly suspicious about that, and passed me to the other one – female, even got egg pouches. *Well, you can forget that – I'm not fertilising them.*

She was a High Senior; no miner this one – that's military uniform. She's from the Aston Navy. Speaks clear Fed – accented, of course, with chirrups.

'The Co-Mans and Krill,' she was telling me, 'are loosely uniting against us across the territory. The Rhoy are undecided – as always. Where does TerraFed stand?'

'You're asking me? How the shugg would I know? It's eight years since I was ignominised out the Corp, and haven't been in TerraFed regions since.'

They had some scheme up their orifices, and were wanting to fix a treaty with TerraFed. So they were thinking that maybe I might be a possible way to get things started?

'Me?' I nearly said they must be mad, but they'd have diced me if I did. 'I'm nothing. Ex-everything. Ask my companion.'

'You are more. We have checked on you. You were Fed Space Forces.'

Should I tell 'em how far and hard I was thrown out? I shrugged, *Let 'em find out for themselves.*

'You are to accompany our delegation to Fed Base V at Seraquin. And negotiate a treaty.'

'With you?' This was High Senior Egg-pouches talking; name of Chirrup chirriperty churk chick – or Chicky for short. 'And you want safe passage to Fed Base, with me and Captain Orlea?'

'Not the other human. She stays and works the machine.'

'No. I can't leave her.'

'You must. She works.'

'She's a Corp officer – she would have much more influence that I have.'

'And less conception about the reality of this situation. She must remain. As a hostage.'

'Hostage to what?'

'Our return. Mine and yours. You belong to us. We captured you – we do not give you away – little worth though you have. And for my safe return, as well. How much value will they place on you and your female?'

'On me? None. Less than none – I'm not welcome in Fed lands. Her? You'll have to ask her.' I shrugged, but they don't understand shrugs. It means something else, I think.

I just caught an impression of a glance between them. *Orlea's dead already?* You got to wonder when they eye-flick like that. And they're lying vindictive shykers at the best of times. *Is that why they won't consider her going? They've killed her in their chastisement?*

'I'm going nowhere without her. She's with me. Partners.' Clicky's boyfriend twisted my arm. A lot. More. Double spiral fractures, judging by the pain, angles and cracking-glurking sounds.

Clicky stopped him getting hold of my stump. 'It was one of my brood that you didn't fire on when we first came in. Why not?' Her eye pods dilated.

'I'm a miner, not Corp.' I gave her another shrug that she misunderstood. Shykes! That hurt the hell out the wreckage that was my shrieking screwed-up arm.

'But you handled the laser as a fighter. You could have let the Co-Mans past.'

'Long time ago, I was in the Corp. Thrown out. You don't wanna know why – Well, you're not going to find out from me. I could have let them past? Yes, and then what? An even nastier pack telling me what to do? We wouldn't have lasted two minins with them. At least we know where we are with you. Now, where is Orlea?'

They wouldn't say. 'Cared for,' was all. I had a really dead feeling about that.

It was to happen soon. They were planning, preparing; getting me prepped up, too. Heard them saying kavo'atta something. That was explosive. And izixtra. That was something about the body – false body part; an implant or something like that. So that was interesting.

This senior Aston and I are to be sent to TerraBase V. Right, so one of us might have an explosive implant. Intended as a double-cross? She's suiciding? We'll both be dead, whichever of us has the implant. Maybe just insurance – triggered if she dies? That's been known. Bloody powerful things they have these days.

My left arm is regrowing! Amazing. There's a pink lump extending from the elbow, with five lumpy nobbles on the end.

By the time we got to Base V, my arm was around half-returned and I could twitch the wriggly bits. Just the same, I had no idea what I was supposed to be doing, or how I might warn anyone about possible detonating implants.

"Welcome" was not on the airlock iris, especially when they realised who I was. First thing I got, apart from, 'Oh. It's you. Lannister,' when we were escorted in, was my Corp record loudly quoted to me. As if I wasn't aware of it. "Ejected with ignominy" for refusing to obey orders; cowardice and traitorous activities. Officially, I wasn't allowed on any Terra-held territory, not since the "trial", on penalty of death by airlock. I don't much care – at least it wasn't me who wiped out 101 non-combatant Rhoy. Somebody did, later. And was similarly censured afterwards, for exactly the opposite to what they did me for.

Thus, I wasn't allowed to mix with any of the humans on TerraBase. Instead, High Senior Clicky Chicky kept a close appendage on me at all times. As if TerraFed would ever want to keep me; unless for ritual execution displayed on screens from here to Yeeten, maybe.

The treaty terms were agreed in outline for discussion. Which was pretty much all that either side hoped for – hostilities were ceased. Disputes would be resolved by negotiations. 'Just needs to be signed at the Aston end of the line by their Commissioner of Governance. The signing can be trivi'd and beamed back here.'

It took four days of me being chain-dragged round with Clicky, fed under guard, and kept silent. Then it was all agreed and nodded through, SH Clicky with her eyes and antennae everywhere. TS tight-beam discussions with Base were completed. It was all set to be agreed.

I grabbed an opportunity to haul one of the senior TerraFeds aside while Clicky was diverted on some timescale details. He didn't want anything to do with me. 'Get yourself back, Lannister. You're officially dead, so if you stay here, you know what happens to corpses? They get incinerated or spare-parted. So you'd best go.'

A few others spotted us, came over, telling me, 'Just get the documents signed so the non-aggression and joint access provision comes into effect.'

'You surely don't trust'em? They've crossed the Krill over, and I very much suspect they killed Captain Orlea with the same treatment they gave me. Maybe... maybe not.'

'Of course we don't trust them. Totally self-oriented. They've broken every treaty they've ever signed with the Krill, Rhoy, Kerries. But it's our only chance for a period of peace while we prepare—'

'Sure, that's koh for me. But what about Captain Orlea? She should be released back here if you're fixing any kind of deal.'

'Officially, that's why you're going back – to fetch Captain Orlea. Her father's something big in HQ, so she's important to somebody important. So yours is an Honour Return for the Hostage.'

'She's all you want back? Not me, huh?'

'Get her back, and you could be re-admitted – that's official.'

I looked round the group. 'Why would I want to come back here? To be a non-person among you lot? Maybe I could do something better?'

'Like what?' That was a mix of wondering and derision.

'Chances are, they'll sign, and keep us both there as continuing hostages. I got the silverdust bedded in me now, so I don't care whether I come back or not. But I have to try to get Captain Orlea back. I feel responsible for her, after I pulled the Krill off her in the first place and kept her alive since.'

'They're not known for keeping their word, or live hostages.'

'I know that. Perhaps I could do something else?'

'Oh…?'

So I was batted back to Farnside Aston Base with Senior Clicky. All I had to do was collect Orlea, and get her back – or at least keep her safe until the first Terra units arrived to begin the Shared-Surface Arrangement.

'Your companion? She is gone.' The first senior Aston I saw was their usual brutal, straight-in-the-gut type.

What? Scruggit. Like I hadn't known. But hearing it like that really scrugging hit me. 'What do y' mean, *Aston?* She can't be gone – she was the hostage for—'

'Of course. But we would say anything to you under those circumstances. She was passed on to the Co-Mans in our discussions with them. As a gesture of goodwill. So I expect she is long-dead – the Co-Mans really don't understand the idea of live prisoners.' I think he was laughing, but they don't do that.

'But… Why? I mean. We had—'

'She was of no further significance to us. Only to you. You are also of no further value to us. Nor to your own people, we understand. We have the treaty, and non-aggression agreement from TerraFed. It will be signed very shortly. The communication has been sent to Central. The female's importance was nil the moment you left for TerraBase. And *you* are of no consequence now you are returned here.'

That about Orlea was a dead believable alternative. And about me. I'll be in the bin before the first Terrans arrive. I was sick about Orlea. *I bet she blamed me. The scruggers – to treat her like that!* To hand her over to the Co-Mans! Shikit! It didn't bear thinking about, if she'd even been still alive then.

Got to pull myself together. *Mon't lose my hair. It needs to be done calmly. If only for Orlea, and myself.* 'Tell me, *Aston*, the izixgia kavo'atta that high Senior Clicky had?' I can tell when they're shocked – their palps tremble. He was *very* shocked.

'How do you know?'

I ignored him. 'How potent was it? Enough to destroy the TerraFed control complex? The whole of TerraBase V? Triggered by her? or by her death?'

Ah, yes, I was in the right orbit there. Couple of other senior Astons had come in, listening, flexing their abdominal mandibles.

'So what do you reckon, *Aston?*' I can say that in a really insulting tone. 'Think you're good with detonation implants? How good do you think Fed implants are? You've heard of Multi-Access Chain Reaction bombs, have you?'

Ha! Bit of frill-pursing there. Good, they'll understand, then. 'When one detonates, there's no explosion. It's merely a powerful broadcast of multi-access codes. Seeps into anything electronic in range – no shielding stops it. It creeps. It affects the metal. It sits there and waits for the second-phase trigger.'

They stayed blank-eyed. 'So? What does it do? Spy on our communications? We can block that easily enough.'

That genuinely made me snuff a chuckle, 'Ha... No, *Astons*. When the second phase is triggered, everything in transmission range that has a metallic valency will have absorbed some of the basic coding, and will begin to accelerate its heat absorption properties. Eventually, a continuous reaction will set in. Everything metallic *eriyecek* – will start to warm up. Until it melts, and shortly afterwards explodes. This base, for example, would be utterly destroyed within hours if the reaction were to be triggered.'

They were looking a mite edgy then, pincers twitching, like they wanted to mash and mince me. *You want to do that, anyway.*

'This base; and most of the planet with it, I imagine. Quite slowly, might take a slow creep away from here, days, maybe. Never been tried with a planet-based setting before. Certainly anything metal would self-vaporise eventually. In theory, even the ores in the ground. Enough heat to melt the planet would eventually be generated.'

'And this bomb...?' One queried. *Yes, their palps are on quiet overtime now. Made you think, huh?*

'Is within me. It is triggered by my specific thoughts, or my death. Now, *Astons*. You have one perio to bring Orlea to me, unharmed. Or you will all cease to exist.'

'And you as well,' the big one with a crooked proboscis countered, rather pathetically.

'Me? I ceased to exist ten years ago, when I refused orders. Nobody survives that: I've been on borrowed time thereafter. I knew my time was beyond its keep-till date long before your craft caught us mining. I imagine it's why I didn't fire – let you kill me. Disappointing that you didn't do it then.'

I could see their minds zipping and clicking over, 'And what would stop you triggering the device?'

'You let me go, with Captain Orlea, then any broadcast would only affect the vessel I was travelling in.'

'How do we know—'

I put a hand up to my mouth – universally recognised as the Shut-up sign. 'Any attempt to forcibly move me off-planet will result in automatic release of the broadcast; so will my death; or the end of one perio without my coding. Yes, of course it can still be stopped – by Orlea's appearance here in,' I checked, 'three hours. If she's alive, you can get her here – or at least on the screens. If, not, you can kiss your carapaces goodbye, *Astons*.'

I allowed them time. Long enough for it to sink in. To contact their base; their home planet, probably; to get in touch with the Co-Mans or whoever. All fruitlessly. To scuttle round and not come up with a living Orlea, or even a screen-alive one.

They returned, no doubt having spent the time plotting with their Base and anybody else they could think of. Now, almost bragging of their failure to locate any word of Orlea; and my impending extremely protracted doom. 'We detect no trace of any transmission device within you. You are bluffing.'

'Koh, *Aston*. Have you heard of a systems virus called a MAT? A Multi-Access Trigger? No? It's the Multi-Access part of Chain Reaction. You remember I mentioned that? Good.

'Right. When I entered here, straight off the ship and out the airlock, do you recall the first thing I said? No? Well, it ended in *"Aston"*. Loud and clear. That began the sequence. The code is doubtless thoroughly embedded in all your metallic, electronic and nanotronic materials and equipment. It's there, biding its time. I've said it aloud four more times? Maybe five. Each time reinforces the embedding. The sequence is in motion. I told you to look after her, to have her here. I shall have to apologise to her for my failings when we meet in the Great Orbit...'

Somehow, their chitinous visages betrayed a lack of understanding.

'Allow me to explain. The coding is a virus. It embeds itself into Systems systems. It is self-perpetuating. It propagates itself through any kind of System communication. So if, in the past three hours, you've had any contact whatsoever with any other ships, bases or planets, then the MAT virus will have accompanied your messages and found somewhere snug to settle, in each receiving system. If those receivers have had any wider contact, then the virus will have spread again. *And so forth.*'

I think the dawn was coming over them about then. 'Perfectly safe. Unless the trigger within me is, er, triggered. Then the whole chain reaction will commence – and all the others will self-activate. Each one will cause a separate melt-down to begin in its own vicinity. I imagine you've been chatting with all your Central Bases? And the Co-Mans? Yes? Oh good.'

Oh yes, they're getting the idea. 'Your whole civilisation will begin to destroy itself very shortly, hmm?'

Funny how coldly calm I feel. 'You're merely something to be done. Something long overdue – like me.'

'TerraFed would be destroyed, too. You wouldn't—'

'No. Not Terra. You may have noticed that you've received no responses from *any* Terran base for the past day. All Terran communications are cut indefinitely. Strictly limited to ultra-string-coded messages at Top Level One Only. Whole systems physically de-activated – switched off. You could probably have launched a huge – and highly successful – attack in the last few hours.'

'You couldn't do it. You wouldn't.'

'Of course I'd do it, you fools. I've met you. I know you. I tried to trust you. *I* attached a great deal of personal importance to Orlea. You should *not* have let me down. The destruct-coding is now embedded in every piece of your electronics-related metal—'

'Your own people are killing you.'

'Scuff me backwards! You fools! *I* suggested it. I begged TerraBase to let me do it. To fully activate the coding – and melt down your whole empire, I only have to say one word. Just once.'

'And that is?' The ludicrous arrogance was still there.

'*Aston.* You imbeciles. *Aston.*' In that tone of voice. '*Aston.* Now then... The length of time it has been entrenching itself, consolidating, readying itself – this means that when it does detonate, the melting will commence immediately. As I understand the paraphysics, it could be instant, full-heat vaporisation... eh? *Aston?* Ten... Nine...'

Funny how suicide comes so easily when oblivion's beckoned so often and so comfortingly. 'Eight. Seven. Scrugg – you should see the stupid looks on your, er, *faces.* You're finished, *Astons.*

'Two.

'One—'

Whoooommmmphhhhh....

CONTINUUM

'Kenni, I've just received confirmation over the inset. Our comrades arrive today.'

Syrah turned and wraithed across the space, twirling a pair of ethereal tendrils and reforming them as temporary Earth-style arms-cum-wings while she engaged in an energy-absorption spread in the sun.

'Are we prepared?' she asked. 'We're sure our proposals are viable? And we're ready to firm them up into definite plans, with all the organisational matters?'

'Three years in the planning, Syrah. Yes, it's been long enough. We have this planet sized up. This is no time to panic or have doubts.'

'It will be good to have other Fantasmas to speak with, join with. No disrespect, Kenni, but it will refresh my cloudellas to vary my circle of acquaintants for a time. We must both be tired of exchanging each other's peritoids so often.'

'Indeed. Shall we meet them here?' She cast a vision ceptor around the glorious snow-capped mountain peak that they most commonly frequented. 'Or one of the empty cathedrals we've been looking at? Or a temple?'

'Mmm. That could be quite appropriate, in view of our suggestions.'

'I so look forward to hearing all the gossip about Wraitheen: they may have news of my own wisplets, and how things are in Nuanca.'

'I don't imagine they've had the trials and tribulations we've endured these past years.'

'Oh, come on, Kenni, the humans have had their entertaining moments; be fair.' She reached across the snow face and curled a newly-forming fingerettes into a twist with a similar one that Kenni was already forming.

The locatrons brought their friends to them at the colossal temple in the desertlands, and they drifted together, luxuriating in the newness of each other's company and their tales of home, and Earth and the other planets they knew. Soaking in the sun and the warmth and light, bathing in the oxygen, enjoying the sheer pressure of the atmosphere, and the gravity.

'Heavenly,' they agreed.

'Ahh, that brings me to the business, Myona. Heaven is a favourite concept of these humans. They're very susceptible to suggestions, such as the whole concept of Heaven, The Continuum, Pwaradice, and the like. Every segment of the planet has its own ideas of these other-worldly existences. Nibbanha… Empyreum.'

'They have whole buildings and complexes such as this one; and thought systems based entirely on imaginary creatures or beings,' Kenni interrupted, in his eagerness. 'They spend enormous sums of wealth and time building ridiculous notions and beliefs around The Eternal Continuum. Humans create both mental premises and physical ones in the form of elaborate buildings.'

'Such as this,' Syrah spun around the great temple, with its magnificent complex of towers and spires; huge halls and broad plazas; domes and minarets.

'Quite often, their ideas entirely lose credibility in the face of the blindingly obvious. Just look at some huge expensive buildings that stand empty and unused.'

Kenni conjured up enormous holographic images of soaring cathedrals, towering churches and sky-reaching statues.

'Mmm,' their new companions looked on, bemused, and had a brief relaxation and stretch, intertwining among the colonnades alongside Syrah and Kenni. 'The Continuum, hmm?'

'Sometimes, they take on greater inner strength; generally because their leaders wheedle and twist and betray and mis-portray their ideals. They're the ones with most to lose, comfort and power-wise; and most to gain if they manage to convince the populace of an bliss-filled afterlife. The people become inspired to great things, with these visions of themselves soaring divinely through the Continuum of all TimeSpace.

'Thus, it's not hard to con most of the people most of the time?' Liriop was grasping the idea of this at once.

'Not difficult at all,' Syrah smugged a wraithing arm. 'Very simple, in fact. We've tried it ourselves, and been remarkably successful. All we do is appear to them in our basic ethereal form, and mooch round, poking into a few heads, giving them visions of idyllic paradises. We seek out some of the most susceptible humans to become our chosen few—'

'Balance-deficient individuals.'

'They're so easy to persuade with a few twists and curling visions, and they're eager to do the work for us.'

'They convince others of our reality and our wondrous intentions; and spread our dreams and visions of wonderful futures somewhere in the heavens. Yes, up in the skies, in mystic places. We find it's best to keep locations vague.'

'We have,' Syrah resisted the urge to smug and smirick again, 'carried out a number of experiments along these lines, and encouraged them to persuade each other to—'

'What? Fight each other for space in the heavenly place?'

'No; they do enough fighting already – one delusion-mad group against another.'

'No, we guide them towards joining us, following us. They call us gods – and we embellish and encourage them with an occasional extra vision and a bit of locational guidance. They follow directions and coordinates so obediently. We can get a mass of them to collect together somewhere out of sight of their fellows, and beg to be taken away.'

'For us to take them away from all this,' Kenni rotated, reformed in the vast spiralling curl of a tornado, and settled back comfortably, delighted with the refreshment of new company after all this time being worshipped by mud-crawling mushies.

'What's the point of that?' The three new Wraitheens were becoming impatient.

'Well, we send a sub-molecular link down in their midst. Then we fancy it up with light patterns and some of Jenlo's music—'

'Yeuk! That shitifferous garbanging crud from Hidiscus? It's appalling.'

'It brings them in,' Kenni smilured. 'These humans really go for its after-life-sounding cadences, or so they say. They come trooping to us, lining up, and we vanish them up a stairway, or down a ramp. Into a container of some kind. and remove them.

'Where to? What for?'

'The processing plant on Simyay, for food supplements, or even as straight-forward, stand-alone foods themselves. The Simyans absolutely relish them mashed, minced, diced... They're trying out a variety of dishes and recipes. The brains are best removed – they make good carretela food, apparently.'

'The humans? You've tried them? Tasted them?'

'A few times. Gnawed on a few that irritated me. Very tasty. Lot of energy packed in them.'

'These humans are an ideal admixture of proteins and fats, minerals, water...'

'Sounds good.'

'And there're no side-effects; no drawbacks, like with the Herats that you have to boil for an age first?' Myona was seeing the possibilities here. 'You reckon there's potential here for harvesting these beings on a bigger, more regular scale?'

'Definitely. We begin by re-encouraging whole populations to believe in us, and The Continuum, and their own specially-reserved, privileged place in Universal SpaceTime. A few appearances; indisputable visions of us looking very much like their most popular thoughts of what their gods look like. Then we can encourage batches of them to congregate in these old buildings – churches, cathedrals, temples, all kinds of edifices where they like to come and worship us, and revive the whole silliness—'

'There are plenty of localities around this planet where the primitive beliefs are still in favour of things like us ruling their lives. They love being ordered round and bullied by non-understandable, non-existent beings. Except, we have the distinct advantage of actually existing, and can manifest ourselves however we wish –

or however they dream. We merely need to nudge their thoughts towards mental slavery, drooling in our wake, and peaceful co-existence – we don't want our livestock killing or eating each other, do we?'

'And there's a whole planet-full? Properly managed, we should be able to encourage a high and balanced birth and harvest rate – push it as some super-science rationale with their religions—'

'Like a new interstellar reality? The New Continuum?' Liriop, Myona and Peesos were becoming caught up in this, 'We can simply seed a bunch here and there with the idea of glory being imminent, and they'll come flocking into the hoppers?'

'Whenever we want to harvest a new batch – perhaps when a new bulk order comes in.'

'Yes, it definitely sounds good – and is certainly practical and worthwhile. We could manage insto-transport batches of around a thousand at a time to Simyay, or Jeelok—'

'Or holding pens on Ghas, in case of glitches when we need rush orders.'

'Yes, I like it. Great work Syrah… Kenni.'

'We'll just need to beef up security at the processing and holding end – wouldn't want any escaping, would we? They'd be like a plague of vermin across the civilised universe.'

'Er,' Kenni hesitated, 'actually…'

JUST VISITING

'You're 60897804 Smith A.'

This skoigogg sat there, all pomp and sideways glance, feet up – that's ill-mannered of him – feet on the table. Brought up in the Bronx, I imagine. Pair of'em lounging in the visitor section. Seems like they're not fussy what kind of visitors they let in these days. But it's still a cage – steel bars and bare floor. Table and chairs screwed down – at least they hadn't hand-cuffed me to the bar across the table like they did when my brief was there those first few times.

I don't come in the visiting section often. Their side's the same barren concrete as ours, identical plastic chairs.

'I know who I am. You fetched me out my cosy cell where I was diligently studying economics, to tell me who I am?' I gave him the sneer, You cheated. You must have asked for me by name, and that's what it says on my chest tab. So you weren't exactly stretching your intellect to come out with that, were you? Or were you?'

I touched my name tab as I sat. Looked at the Pair from the Other Side through the gobbed-up glass. 'Besides, you missed "Prisoner" out. And nobody goes through the whole number – I answer to eight-zero-four.

'I dunno,' I addressed the Gods, 'the idiots who turn up these days.'

'Too fucking obvious to say, isn't it? Everybody your side is a prisoner.' Smirky Boy with silvered glasses – Wearing deep shades indoors! I tell you, talk about a Plank-head.

'What some zleiglers'll do for their idiotic image, huh?' I piss-took and touched my temple. He did the same, realised what I meant about his shades, and that was him screwed off with me already. *Image-conscious, huh? You're on a loser with me.*

'You're the twat on the inside, right? *Skinner?*'

Ha! You come visiting me, so you must want something, and yet you start by insulting me. Twat? Skinner? That's a threat-name. I'm no Paedo. Another black mark there, Plankie.

'One of you better say something worthwhile next, or I'm out of here.' I made as if to rise, 'My celly's got a better line in chat-up. You drag me away from the best cheesecake lunch this side of the Shenandoah to state the obvious.' Like I want anything to do with a pair of mirror-face sholgoths.

'You'd miss what we've got to say.'

'Y' should'a passed me cigs or a cell, not waste my time on chat. *Guard!* These two dicks want me to knock seven-five-two off. You should search'em for a skank.'

Guard Rickyic gave me the blanks. *Never believe a con, huh?*

'Wait. Wait. Come on back. Hear us out.'

Permitting myself a little smile inside, I stopped. 'It better be good, considering the meal I'm down on.'

'There's some new evidence that may have surfaced. On your case.'

'Oh, yeah? Like what? Y' not here to tell me that – not for my benefit. You ain't the type to help anybody.'

'Yeah? How d'you figure that out?'

'You wouldn't have said "may have". If it was definite, you'd have said so. Thus, it's conditional on… what? my cooperation in some matter? If I'm ready to do what you want, then you'll bring up the evidence in a positive light. Otherwise…' I shrugged.

'So y' wanting to use it, if it exists, and use me. So your new evidence either proves I killed them three shikoles without provocation, and the court'll stretch my eight to the twenty-five they mentioned at sentencing. Or it proves I was totally justified in de-lifing'em, and I'm out of here free. So which is it? And what's your stake in it?'

They gave each other the smarmy look, like they met wise guys before. 'We're here to help.'

'Sure you are – yourselves and whoever sent you.'

Another glance.

'You can bend the story either way, huh? Eye witness changed their mind? New one suddenly remembered? What? That Renshaw did have a gun? One of the drinkers pocketed it?'

Give'em credit – they had the grace to look mildly surprised; amused, too. But it ain't hard to figure some things out, not when you're surrounded by cons in the Pen. The seated one waved me back down. 'We know you weren't born in Alaska—'

'Born? I grew up in England, Europe. Never been near Alaska. Getting arrested and charged with three counts of murder, a month after I arrived in the States kinda limited my travels here. I been in the slammer since. Stitched up by you lot. Fix the foreigner, huh? Get a conviction the easy way.'

He didn't even have the grace to look guilty. 'Sure, I'm with the Law,' he said, 'but I don't know anything about all that.'

My look of disbelief just made him sneer. *Shite-wipe. You don't get it, do you? Last chance I'm giving you.* I waited. He sneered again. I was out.

'It's Dr Zeit who wants to talk with you. He—'

I saw them panicking as Guard pulled my cuffs and legs back tight. 'Sod off,' I shouted as the door closed behind us.

It was two weeks before they made the second attempt – I was pissed with that. They should'a done better – some guys in here get the idea you're informing if you get unknown visitors, and two weeks is a long time to put up with the repercussions. But today would be quicker if there weren't no instant benefit without strings.

It was just the other guy; the supposed doc – Zeit. Guard nodded, and he slid a couple of packs across. 'They been checked.'

Yeah, they'll get checked again. Or confiscated, as we call it in here. 'What is it you come for?'

He stared at me for maybe five seconds. Just long enough to get me deciding I was leaving.

'Okay, okay,' he waved me to sit down again. 'You got your smokes; so hear me out. There's some cell footage turned up on the net. Like a laughline.'

'Huh?'

'*This* kinda site.' He held his cell up, playing some rednecks setting off firecrackers up each other's backsides.

I stared back. 'Y' boring me. I ain't bored in here, don't need this. I'm enrolling in a survival course this afternoon.'

'A little patience, Smith.' At least he missed the 804 off.

'So say something to keep me here.'

'*This* footage is you, in action against the three guys you killed in Delaney's Shamrock—'

Bush-faced IRA fundraisers by the looks and sounds of them. They detected a trace of England in my accent. I mean, *me?* What have I got against the Irish, Yiddish or Radish? What I got was a glassed face and gut and they got throats ripped open. No witnesses in a crowded bar. Nobody left in the place by the time the cops turned up. And there's my three guys lying there, emptied of the red stuff.

'That's New York's Finest for you, missed the ferry again – bled out in under a minute all told. But me, I was two hours getting to the emergency room, the extra-long way round – the yellow cab route, like they say. Now don't get me wrong – I'm quarter Irish. Grandfather from Athenry. Often went back as kids – Galway, all that region and coast. Loved it; loved the people. "My people," like Gramps used to say, and I used to echo it.'

This Zeit guy just gives me the stare like he don't hear any of it.

'But somebody was more than happy to stitch me up – not too good on stitching my face, though, huh? That's why it's such a mess.'

Zeit? He's still giving me the tolerant look that's fading quick, so I gets cheesed with him, 'Look, just tell me what you're here for, Doc. This ain't gonna be any good for me, is it?'

He gives me the deadeye and shows me some more footage from a cellphone. 'Somebody in the bar, standing by the juke box. Here. See...'

I watched. Crap stability, camera all over the place. But there I was; and the bothersome three. Them rousting me. Me getting glassed. I'm being jerked all over. So's the camera. Then I'm suddenly not there any more. There's a blur. Then nothing – I've vanished.

These three are going down. Yeah, I recall, alright. Seemed at the time like they went down real, real slow. But on here, on the footage, they just dropped, like normal. It was me whose timescale had changed – I was moving too fast to film.

Zeit the Slimeball was smiling at me. I really ain't stupid. I know that look. He imagined he had me snaffled over a barrel. Thought he had me intrigued, not giving credence what I'd just seen. But I ain't baffled or interested, or surprised or disbelieving. None of them things. I know what happened.

It's you who's desperate, Zeit, not me. You believe you're on to something with me. You think you have a use for someone who can move that fast, huh?

'A scrap of cell footage won't get me outa here, Zeit. Don't mean a thing, far as the DA's concerned. So speak. And make it *very* good.'

'That vanishing? Ultra-speed? If you could control it, you could be outa here anytime you want. So how come you're still inside this place? You don't have control of it? Maybe don't even know about it?'

OK, so you've cottoned on to my speed thing, huh? Hyperspeed. So... I gazed at him in blank mode. *Take it easy, eight-oh-four. We don't want this getting out – it'd explain too much that's happened in here. There'd be a lot of blaming looks in my direction, and I need this refuge for a time longer.*

'Or... You can do that any time you want?' He said again. 'And you choose not to. So can you?'

'What if I could?' *Pretend to negotiate... find out what he believes he knows.*

'Ah.' He sat back, entering parleying mode. 'We might have work for you.'

'OK, Doc. Cut the shite. Don't give me no BS. Just tell me what you want.' He was about to smirk. Changed his mind.

'Join us. The US Government.' A smug, fait accompli look on his visage.

'As what? Assassin? Thief? Spy? They're the obvious uses for someone with such an ability.'

He shrugged, smiled, thought he'd got me. Sure... but it'd be forever; they'd keep me indefinitely – other uses, research, whatever. Worse, they'd know about me. Might even find out about my other talents. Can't have that.

I need another year safely in here before the Glaxia InterStellar Warrant on me runs out. If I'm incarcerated, anywhere at all, the Law Officers in the StellarFed ain't allowed to get at me to enforce the warrant.

But, after January 4th next year, they can't touch me, even by Glaxia Time Counting; even if they're waiting outside the gates. Then, I can let myself out, free of StellarFed harassment. After all this time dodging them across the vac – twenty-eight years – they'd still get me for what I did on Headray.

But. I'm not leaving now; certainly not Zeit's way. I'll stick to my own timescale and agenda. I only need to keep my head down in here, out their clutches and claws, pincers and stingers, teeth and tentacles, for one more year.

'You gotta leave, Doc. You're out your depth here.'

He was reluctant about letting me go, but me and Guard went one way, and he stayed there, looking pissed.

One more year snugly inside, I'm smiling at him as I get the shackles fitted, and you, my turdy slow-arsed, dim-witted little planker, will be right in my cross-hairs. And so are the cops and prosecutors who stitched me up and stuck me in here – even if it did work out very nicely, self-protection-wise.

Then I'll turn my attention to the rest of this shitty little planet. Remiss of me, I know, but when it came to looking things up in my dictionary, I never did understand "mercy".

CHITS

Another grubby town. Another scorching, dry day. *Another desert dump on this eternal pit of a planet.*

The dust rose in hot little swirls round my feet, made worse by the Chitterbugs that played or danced or whatever they were doing on the sidewalks and in the road. A tight chasing pack of them came hurtling from one side-alley after another, nearly knocking me over a couple of times. Then stopping and spinning as though it was my fault. Chittering like giggling little maniacs. Chits are nuisances wherever you find them, so they say. Me, I don't know'em that well. It's just what folk say.

Took me back a time, though… *Chits racing round, all clicking like a street full of ticker machines on double speed.*

'Kack-*tie*,' I blasphemed, just mildly. The heat of the day I can do without. *It was hot like this, that day before… Sun's near vertical, and this backpack's as wearisome as every other aspect of this dreary dry little town. What am I doing here?*

I wandered in the wilting heat.

"For Sale" on a building, written in Chit – I always thought it meant "Salt", till I clanged with a seller – A salt seller – get it? Never mind. I really did believe that sale meant salt in Chit, but I forgave myself – it's not an alphabet or language I was familiar with at the time.

But I know now; it means "Do you want to buy it?"

I sat in the shade for a moment, powered my Cari up, and did an i-web search. Found out about this place – the building, the town. Just an excuse to shade myself a moment or two longer. I looked it up and discovered this wilting, bleached-out structure was exactly what I didn't know I really wanted. So the Cari advert said as the tiny screen lit up; a "buyer-tunity", apparently. Something to buy and make a profit on.

Looking at this edifice that was giving me shade, and reading about it on the camara DV, it was like a personal invitation – advertising for *me* to come and look. Some places and Cari-pages are good like that – they grab you. Most aren't.

Ah, what the Pit... The dust-bleached plastic façade sure isn't promising.

Nor was the interior when I went in. 'What's for sale, exactly?' I asked.

'Everything. I'm leaving.' The old feller wasn't old; he was just desert-faded, like the whole place.

Sure, it's bright-lit inside – that's the solar panelling on overtime; but it's just as hot as the streets – that's the heat exchange on strike. The place had an unfriendly feel to it, so I was re-thinking. But they'd all be the same, if they were even open. The lukewarm drink was weak, and the glass dirty.

The window seat almost beckoned. It was the only one where the table had been cleared, so that one it was, with its depressing view across the road, the Chitters still going at it in the dust, circling and dashing, arguing, or fighting, ganging up.

It became quite absorbing, I never had occasion to watch them at length before – not for yonkeys' years, anyway. A little one – not much over my mid-thigh height – seemed to be organising the others – huddled together like a pack of bugs, all heaving carapaces and wings aflutter. Yes… it had a slightly green tinge, so it was female. And very glossy – so she looked after herself. *She's probably drug-running from that bench in the median strip down the middle of the road,* I decided.

Anywhere else, the median would have been grass, shrubs, trees, but in Trentwin, it was a mix of sand, dust and litter.

On the other hand, watching them longer, they're Chits – who knows what goes on their heads. *Perhaps they are selling salt.*

The door clattered open, and a couple of them chittered up to the counter, asking for drinks. The tender ignored them. Then he came round to offer them a kick if they didn't clear off. 'They always wanna pay in Chit money,' he gruntled. 'No good to me.'

He showed me a coin when I asked.

'That's the stuff?' I checked it on my teeth – hard. 'Good quality metal. I'm getting a taste of Hiridum?'

'Dunno,' he shrugged. 'I eat boogers and flits, not coins.'

'Interesting, though,' I said. 'Wanna sell me a couple? They do different ones? Sizes? Motifs? I know a guy – woman – who collects such things.'

Yes, he did have others.

I tried the four different coins in a PortoTesta in the back of my Cavan. The spectral analyser showed organics as well as mineral elements, and all four coins were consistently decent quality.

Ten mins on the Cari and I had an idea of their value on the Sedex market, as bullion. Couldn't find anything about their rarity value as collectors' items. Nobody wanted Chit coins – including the Barky who wouldn't serve Chits if they wanted to pay in these.

So I went back to the bar to check a few more things with him.

He was pied off, 'Town's run down. Most humans have left. The Chits have always been here; they're natives to the area. They're no real bother, don't work, so never have real money to spend.' He looked like he might clean a few glasses, but just wiped them with his apron and re-shelved them.

'A few Zoeys have moved in,' he started again, 'the Hemizoans, but they don't seem to be doing too well farming. They're having bother digging wells for the aquifer irrigation, and they're growing stuff for the Chits – who can't afford to buy it.'

There's got to be a niche here, I'm thinking, *people leaving; population changing. Must be a gap for something.*

So Barky keeps up his great line in optimism, 'The mine's petered out, plus the farm produce market's falling. Chits are staying, doing subsistence foraging. Zoeys are moving in. Great for a town, huh? More full of garbage every day. Won't last much longer.'

Let's look up Zoeys. What do they like that they haven't got here?

According to the Cari, they're farmers who specialise in perrimin fruits of various kinds. For export, I imagine. *Hmm, trying to grow for the Chits and exports? Failing at both?*

And the Chits? What they want in here is a drink, but can only pay in their own coinage, which Barky refuses to accept. They seem to tolerate the heat – they're out there playing. Unless they're adults, in which case, I've no idea what they're doing. They drink So-sode – when Barky'll let'em have it. Wonder what they eat?

'Do you serve the Chits?'

'Roasted and boiled,' he grumbled.

'No wonder you're not making it pay. Tub of laughs, aren't you?'

'They don't want much we got, but yeah, when they got spendable cash, I serve'em.'

'Kay. I'll wander awhile, look around, ponder over it.'

The middle of the road was like a beehive of waist-high crusty-backs and wingies – they're the same, really – different metamorphic stage. Or maybe they alternate, or choose according to mood. I ought to have looked that up before; or remembered better. Never mind – think on the wing, as they say. Or on the crusty-back.

So I went walking into the road bearing this tray – the Chits were actually occupying the least-necessary roadway refuge I've ever seen – traffic volume amounts to nil while I've been there. Greeny-Glossy is in the middle, holding court. They see me coming and slow down, some move back, others stand in a line like an armoured barricade. You feel awful vulnerable like that – all these razor-mouths at just the right level to emasculate you at the drop of a trouserleg.

So I bent, and then knelt, down at their height. 'Brought you a drink.' And put the tray down – twenty flasks.

'Wojjerwant?' GG asked, ignoring the gift when the others overcame their reticence.

'A chat?'

'About?' Sweet little tinny sort of voice.

'Things. Come inside? There's a couple cooling for us.'

I presume it was a suspicious look she gave me. My wife used to do a lot of that – must be a universal expression women can put on. But she nodded, I think, and came with me.

'Barky, the drinks please,' and we sat back at the window table. She sat on it, actually, and whistled for something.

Barky brought a top to clip over her flask. 'Chits knock-em over sometimes, clumsy sods.'

I could see why she needed the clip-on top – she had this proboscis that extruded from the gnashy bit, and I don't think she could see where the end was. It was waving round, and flicked over the flask a couple of times before homing in. 'Ta,' she mumbled when I held it still – the flask, not her prob.

Silent sucking. *She's on best behaviour*, I thought. *Ought to get some heavy-based flasks, or stick-down ones.*

We got down to business, 'If I was in charge of this place, what would you want to see different?' That was about the nub of it.

'Service, manners, cold drink. Nuyuks, petris, fruits, stick biscuits…' She had a mental list of the place's deficiencies and trilled them in a verbal blur.

'And you'd want to pay in your own coinage? What rate? UniCred to yours, I mean? Fairest to do it by weight, because your coins are different sizes.'

She was flummoxed by a question like that – hadn't occurred to her before, except in some vague one-for-one thought in her mind.

'By weight and size would suit me well,' I said. 'Suppose we do a rate of one UniCred for the small size you make, and work out a weight-rate for bigger ones? That seem fair?'

It did indeed.

'To be honest with you, GG, I can sell your coins as metal. And I'd be making a better profit. It would save my meltage costs; there'd just be storage and delivery charges. Higher profit margin would allow me to get more stuff in for you to buy, and make more money out of you – just so you know. So if you want to think about selling me a block of it – an ingot or two…?'

She wasn't looking enthused.

'But if you're oaky with paying the regular price for the regular coins,' I went back a stage, 'then I'd be okay, too. Think about it.'

'Don't need to think.'

'Something else occurs to me. Your coins have a 67% content of Hiridium, which is what I'd particularly want. And Hiridium veins often contain crystals— Yes, of Cortite… You do? And you have? Yes, I'd be interested in looking at anything like that, too.'

She was all gleaming carapace and a second extra-cold drink then.

'I'll just go talk with Barky, see if I can adjust his mind about the price on this place, without cheating him.'

And she went out to discuss matters with her druggie crowd, or whatever they were.

Barky came down on his initial asking price, but I didn't push him much. I negotiated with GG for three of her friends to clean the place up, paying them in cold drinks, and UniCreds for other stuff they might want to save up for.

I kept asking them what they wanted, and their ideas expanded as they thought beyond the drinks being ever-colder – they were checking up on Absolute Zero last time I asked.

A few sessions on the Cari-screen, and I started suggesting things they didn't know they wanted.

'Yes,' I happily confessed to GG, 'I'm trying to create customer demand. Which means you're all getting more things. Some people like to say their standard of living is rising, but that's a matter of opinion. You could view it as losing what cultural heritage you have now.' My turn to shrug, 'Up to you.'

The bar-cum-diner became a cum-shoes and clothes store with background music. Then had to become a music-player seller, too. Plus take-away hot, chilled and packeted foods – they never bought any before! Never knew about them or had the cash.

So – confession time – I'm raking it in. The Hiridium is good quality, and evidently quite plentiful. They were convinced I was the mug, and I knew I wasn't taking them for a ride – doing a profit-share. I've heard about mugged populations biting back with a vengeance. That's not for me – you really should see the teeth on these Chits.

On their own, they forage for minerals to make the cash and some little implements and decorations; collect berries, roots and mushrooms; lead occasional human groups who want to climb and explore; and burrow for their homes – like huge warrens. The alloy they make the coins of is a by-product of their home-extensions. And it in turn has a by-prod in itself – gem quality cortite. They don't bother with it, but it's an interactive organo-mineral that gathers light and stores it, and when it gets overfull – this is the simple version for the likes of me – the light bursts out in "coruscating beams of brilliance". There's a big demand for it, especially after I put Mickley the Marketeer on the case.

'While you're wondering what extension to dig for your granny next, you might think about digging for water? for the Zoeys? They're crap at digging wells out here – amateurs.'

What I got out of that idea was richer customers among the Chits and the Hemizoans – because they could grow their crops better, and the Chits could buy them.

Town was starting to regrow from the inside; there was money around. Couple of other stores opened, just small. Except the bar-diner that opened up two doors down. Sure, competition's healthy, but this place was selling sub-stuff at lower prices than me, getting the trade…

Fair enough on the quality, I told Yaclun when he came round gloating. 'People'll find out and realise.' But he wanted us to come to an arrangement, no inter-aggression.

'No way,' I told him, and started on about feeling a bit responsible for the local Chits.

I lost more customers the following decs. GG wouldn't say what the prob-dicky was. Started avoiding me.

All my pleas and attempted chats might as well have been in Kloj. *Ah well,* I figured, *you'll find out and be back.*

Except she didn't. More of them stopped coming. I saw some lounging round the verandas and sidewalks – and the median dust-walk where GG started. They hadn't been doing that since I came. Clothes scruffier, too.

I felt terrible about killing Yaclun one night, with his harridan wives. Burning their bar-diner down was easy, and the intensity of the fire was clearly the result of the re-ethylised alcohol they had stored, for lacing the drinks they sold to the Chits. *Anything for profit, some people.*

Nobody'll ever know where I got the alky from, or how I managed to seed their place with a store of it; and I only felt terrible for a few minutes.

Some Chits started coming back; others died. Those beetards really had been selling something deadly – something a lot worse that re-eth. So the trouble there was that I didn't know what my Chits had become addicted to; and couldn't get any kind of anti-dote. So it was hard-duck or die for them.

GG was too smart. She thought it was me; blamed me for the deaths. 'All I did was burn him out; I dumped the re-eth in there to burn better, and to make it obvious he was 'dulterating your stuff with something,' I protested, 'I didn't put anything in your drinks or smokes; and I don't know what he was actually giving you.'

But she wouldn't have it, and I really didn't want to kill her. I did my absolute best not to, but she made it increasingly difficult, rallying her people against me. *Killing her's my only option – she's gone astray herself, somewhere along the drugline. But what the crud am I doing here if I start killing the good guys? I'd rather go under than do anything drastic with her, of all of them.*

The virus was guff-awful. Got me among the first tranche – but I'm the wiry hard-bite kuck-awkward sort who wasn't giving way to anything, not in my own town. So I was picking up and wishing I had somebody to look after me and the shops and the business and the Chits and… and everything. But we got a God for that, only she's been discredited with all the kuck-ups this last twenty years. Could do with her now – Matre-Gaia.

The Chits who went down with it weren't doing so well, so I was getting the blame for starting it deliberately and spreading it among them. Everything had gone bollo-shaped.

There wasn't a thing I could do about it, except get slowly better and re-open the bar and hope. I would'a prayed except I don't do that kind thing. Not this past twenty years.

So, naturally, it didn't get any better. I improved, marginally. But the diner-bar was looking – I have to be honest – almost like it did the day before I bought it. I got a couple of my long-time Chits to re-clean everything, and re-start the drinks. Plus two more to run the food – the cash side as well as the prep and serving. It took six days for six Chits to do the place, but they did it well, and were cheaper than I'd charge for my own services.

So it got like a tiny mini-recovery after the virus began to recede and they seemed to be thinking it maybe it wasn't me who'd started it. GG came, not so G&G as she once was, and maybe she was embarrassed. I don't know. But she was all hesitant and saying the first virus victims had been regulars with Yaclun and they thought it could have weakened their resistance against the bug.

I knew we were never going to get back to how things had been – she blamed me too big and too deep for all sorts of things. But we started rebuilding, and had Chits everywhere doing the work and I kept saying, 'This's just making them workers for the daily bag of breath; not free playabout spirits.'

'Times move on,' she said. That was the one time she sat next to me and leaned on me. And I had a drink and she had a sip of dron and we just sat. Would have been quite an occasion if the sun had been setting, or rising, but it was a scorchingly uncomfortable mid-afternoon. Felt good, though.

It was merely business after that. I assumed she remembered everything from before, but didn't want to relive the early days. Like a dream had died inside and this was merely a rerun of an old viddy. Things built up – more at a distance – I didn't have the veezazz inside any more – not that I felt it before, but I feel its absence now I'm not doing much more than following the dots.

Killing a couple of overly avaricious rivals came much easier and quieter next time. And the time after. I employed a pair of Zoeys as general eyes and ears, and I got them a rigout like a uniform and they were accepted as guardians of the law. Except it was my law, which said you died if you attempted to cross me. The only ones who tried it were humanics, and a Zoey.

So, outsiders picked up the idea it wasn't necessarily healthy to come and try to skug Trentwin about. I didn't need to enforce matters after a time; the rules were self-enforcing, and I was seeing more where I'd gone wrong. So I got the Zoeys involved more in town as well as round the farms and hills. Set up a trading post where Yaclun's had been, benefitting from the increasing traffic coming through... and the export trade.

It was really weird when I got drunk some nights, and there was always somebody got drunk with me – couple of humanics who I let come into Twentin and set up legit businesses. But more often it was Zoeys who seemed to have a predilection for booze; and Chits who seemed to see it as a competition to see who could pass out the deepest.

But it wasn't too often, and it seemed to make them comfier with me. Like I wasn't just the bad bossman on the socio-cultural horizon any more. Not all the time, anyway; and I was more comfortable like that. Like being the lead shefter in the woolly herd. Instead of the shef-herder.

Yes, I half-lay on the front board some evenings – on my lounger, not the actual boards. And folk come wandering past, and some acknowledge me, and it's peaceful. And I'm prosperous. More than when I'd come here, anyhow.

Is this what I wanted?

Had I wanted anything when I first came here? Will this do? What? Compared with my dream?

Don't be stupid – I had no dream.

Did I? When I arrived here?

Was it to get away from Androi Heights? To replace them? Impossible? To forget that place? Equally impossible.

To make up for it?

No. Androi Heights wasn't my fault. It simply fell on me, as the priest of Matre-Gaia when the quake had struck. And the Heights had fallen in shuddering, dust-raised ruin, and every dwelling in town had been levelled and pulverised. Except mine.

No amount of re-building or rehoming could ever make up for Androi Heights, and the message I'd spread the day before: 'You are following a path of sloth and delinquency and will be struck down, as I strike down this décor of cakes.'

I knew that ramming my fist down through the cakes and the stand wasn't a great idea, but I was frustrated with them and myself, and it was very theatrical.

Yeah. What a Pit of a bad choice that had been. The cake-stand was modelled after the school. The school where most of the deaths occurred. Sixty-three children – humanics, Hemizoans, Hominids and Chitterbugs.

Except it looked like the Chits weren't included in the first casualty lists I announced. The casualty officer had simply not scribbled the word Chits, down, alongside the names of the four dead, like they had with the other species. Simple mistake in the rush and confusion. I didn't notice – Chit names are so distinctive, it don't need to be said what species they are.

But they thought I was implying that Matre-Gaia didn't count Chits as being important enough to include.

I had let her down; and I'd let the Chits down.

They knew it. I knew it.

Ever since, I've been avoiding all thought of it. Until I came here. And that pack of Chitterbugs had nearly knocked me over out here on the street. Just the same as a pack of Chits had done at that school, that morning... what is it? Twenty-three years ago now.

I'm not looking for salvation. Not looking for anything. But I hope Matre-Gaia might notice me again if I'm more at peace inside. Maybe that's what I'm working on. That, and the chittering little ghosts seem to become quieter, more distant, every time I get myself another drink.

BREACH: LEVEL 2

'Yocks! Look at—' Styne was flibbered to near speechlessness.

'Oh, shuggit!' I sagged, staring down the next huge compartment of Black Star. Most of it wasn't there. What remained was tangled wreckage. 'We're in deep.'

I mean, you look down the centre-section of your ship and see a wrecker's mash-up tangle, and you just know. You go empty and weak and jelly-legged and wonder how in the Pit you're still alive.

'Now we know why the alarms woke us, right enough. We're not going anywhere with the ship in this state.'

'Nobody'll come looking. Won't even realise. It's not as if we register flight routes, check in at beacons, or communicate with anyone.'

'That's the thing about smugglers – we don't.'

'No-one'll know, or care what happens to us, Frankk.'

'We're in the do-do vac alright.'

'Along with a thousand-plus religious escapees.'

'Er… have you looked down there? Half that mash-up is people, cryo units and equipment.'

'You think they're all dead, already?' He peered into the mass of wreckage, 'Suppose they must be.'

'Well, I reckon the dead ones won't be doing anything much; and I guess that any survivors won't be starting that colony on whatever they were going to call their new world.'

'Yeah, World Without a Name; just a number. Until this lot gets there and gives it one. Or any other group that beats us to it, I suppose.'

'Just great, huh? Nearly there, and we get a million alarms going off.'

'And we come out of deep freeze to find this.'

Me and Styne, we just stood there at the cracked bulkhead, and peered through the not-too-clear transplaz doorway into the shattered remains of MidSec 3. And did a swift, unpromising survey of the massed-jumble damage again.

'I think it's known as "Breach: Level 2."'

'Yeah?' he says, what's one of them?'

I quoted The Book. '"Breach: Level 2. Major and catastrophic violation of the hull. Ship's structural and internal integrity severely compromised. Any survivors of the immediate event rarely live long enough to be rescued."'

'It's that alright,' Styne agreed. 'We're deep in the vac with this.'

Silent for a moment, we took in the gaping disaster before us, a great contorted mass of room dividers, twisted girders, scrambled machinery, storage units and cryo banks. 'How can the central division of a hundred-year-old X-9 Superfreighter get its hull split wide open, burst out and wrecked while we're all in deep-frozen cryo-sleep?'

'Easy: explosion hole on the starside – *there*. Might have gone right through. Some of the hull's missing.'

'Oh, yeah, I can see red starlines through the hole.'

'We must still be moving at Light SS if the stars are still red streaks. At least we're still driving, not drifting or tumbling.'

We stared into the massed jumble of wreckage, hardly believing. 'All those people. Dead.'

'And us; we're in the same ship. Though we're not quite as dead and done as they are – yet. But... see through the VX piping wreckage? It looks intact beyond there. Like the damage is mostly confined to MidSec 3.'

'The far sections? They're where the family units are housed, aren't they?'

We peered and squinted. 'Yesss... most of that seems to be intact. If not all of it. So maybe there are two groze families still live-frozen. A thousand or more souls, kids included, give or take.'

'Around seven groze persona, yeah. It's this nearest section where the worst damage is, where the religious and temporal leaders were stored.'

'The unattached males, they were in here, too. The whole lot's gone. See along there? Whether something hit us, or something blew, that's where it happened – maybe debris, or a cometoid fragment. Could have been anything; sheer chance.'

'So what do we do, Frankk?'

'Well, for a start, I'm not going to kill myself, no matter what. I never felt suicidal yet, and I'm not commencing now. Especially...' I was peering down among the tangle. 'Look, maybe we still have a chance here. I'm wondering if we might still get to Planet 907, if our speed's not affected. At least we'll get these freezies where they're expecting to get.'

'You reckon? Are you seeing the same mash-up I am? It's a total tangle-gubbs in there. We'll be past it in three blinks at this speed.'

He was always seeing the gloomy side. 'Okay,' I said, 'we need to suit up, work our way through this mess and see what the damage is the far side, with the engines, utilities, stores, whatever else. Looks like we might be able to rig flexitubes through MidSec 3, along *there*. Get past the nitro-tanks. Create a tube-way down to the family cryo units.'

'Beyond the family units, it's their unattached females—'

'Call them women, Styne, they're not just a consignment any longer. From the looks of all this mess, *we* aren't getting back home any more than these freezies and corpses are.'

'You mean we're stuck out here?' Styne can be dim sometimes.

'What I'm saying is: we can maybe get to 907, but turning round and coming back is nil chance. Black Star is a chalk-off. This's the end of our spacelane.'

'But, you really think we might still make it to Nine-Oh-Seven, wherever it is?'

'Just getting there? Maybe. Look, Styne, we need to create a route through this shambles to the other side, and survey the whole drive and utilities sections.'

'Well,' he was thinking about it, 'we know the main drive is functioning, and we have control—'

'But we'll be yoiking lucky if we don't rip Black Star apart decelerating below Light 1.'

'Or manoeuvring to gain a stable orbit, if there's damage to the close-distance impellor systems.'

'Okay, okay,' I had to laugh at all the impending doom we were heaping on ourselves. 'The ship could be ripped in completely separate halves if the impellors aren't balanced. *Could be anything.*'

'So, you reckon, then, that it's fingers and toes crossed?'

No point worrying about things that we have no control over, until they happen. We can't decide anything until we do some suited-up work through there – rig some lines and flexitubes through.'

'And it might all be out of our control, anyway?'

'Exactly. You're getting the idea, Styne, my friend. See over that way? Looks like the landing craft this side are wiped, but the ones the far side might be untouched. We'd only need one, and simply shuttle everybody down in parcels.'

'That'd take forever.'

'Nearly; but it'd be better than being up in orbit for all eternity. We need to check them out first. If there's no lifeboats to get them down, there's no point waking all the passengers up.'

'Suppose we check on the boats, and impellor controls? See how likely they are to hold together and work right? And wake a few passengers? So they can see the mess? They might think we faked it.'

'You're joking? There's probably three thousand mass-tons of mashed and melted metal right in front of you. We will never be able to not-see that morass of machinery. They've only to take one look at that, and they'll believe we haven't faked it. And they don't have to witness it just yet, before we know if we can do anything about it. Let's just leave'em snoozing, hmm?'

'Worth waking a few to help out with the repairs, d'y think?'

'Probably not. I wouldn't trust planet-clod beginners to work in suits in the vac. Too easy to drift away, or slash your suit open.'

'Yes. Course, Frankk, you're right. Like always.'

Five minins muttering and estimating, guessing and air-sucking, and I gave my verdict. 'We've got around a hundred and fifty days to check out the impellors and controls, and the lifeboats and launchers. Then rig up flexitubes through this mess, check the stores, rations, air-con, main motors and everything else. All the time being extremely careful in suits among all that sharp-edged twisted mass. In stark-lit blackness.'

'Yesss...' He had to agree with me there. 'Our work's cut out for us, alright. Er, I was just thinking, Frankk: if we're going to be stuck on a fresh-out-of-clover planet with this bunch of Holy-Moze,' Styne paused in his ongoing survey of the shambles that used to be our pride and toy, 'do you reckon we should bull up on this religion of theirs before we waken any of them? make out we're one of them?'

'What for?'

'Well, if we have to live among them, like groundlings, it might help us to settle in; be more accepted in their community.'

'Listen, Styne, there's two of us. We're males. And as well as the thousand-odd family persons aboard, there are almost three hundred unattached women still alive and well in the cryo banks.'

'And their leaders, and the spare men, are all mashed and dead?'

'Exactly so. With oinks of effort and lots of luck, we're going to be the heroes who bring them safely to their new Heaven. Believe me, we are not going to have any problem settling in, or making out. *Not ever.*'

Mmm. That was quite an enticing, carrot-dangling thought. 'They might even name the planet after us.'

'What? Like Styne'n'Frankk?'

AND TIME GNAWED BY.

The dust of snow on the mountain peaks
Gave note of the summer's end,
And valleys filled and passes blocked.
But the wagon train was caught in there,
In the icy grip of Manitou, the winter God.
Ninety settlers, with horse and stock
Would starve and freeze
With no way out.

The folk in town all prayed for them,
And clung to hope.
The storms came black,
And the snow was deep and frozen hard.
'It's another band that left it late
To try the crossing by Dead Man Pass,
And will pay for it in skin and bone,'
They said.
And time gnawed by

And winter tolled 'til the springtime melts.
Then riding in came a horseman gaunt
On a haggard mount.
'I'm the scout for Widman's train;
Out of Boise, Idaho.
They're coming in, two days behind.
We're four months late,
All souls secure and our faith intact.'

***

The mudslide came in the dead of night
And hit the bridge with awesome might.
It took the tracks and the telegraph,
And swept the Manga train aside.
Far ahead in Terminal Town, they only knew
The train was late; it's long overdue
For the line through the mounts,
As they all knew well,
Was ever at risk when the monsoons fell.

Came the dawn and it brought no word,
And all that day they stared and prayed.
And time gnawed by.
No engines there to send one out,
So heavy of heart they gathered a team
To walk the line for the three-day hike,
Expecting to find a sea of mud.

And the carriages gone in a mass of rails
And bridge supports.
But the silent gloom was shattered then
By the *tick tap tick* of the telegraph key.
'Number Nine is back on line,
Three carriages short,
But we still have a prayer.'

***

A thousand bombers went out that night
To carpet-bomb the industrial side
Of an enemy town.
The pilots and navvies all knew to a man
They had to deliver their load of death

To strike a blow for the freedom of those
At home who prayed all night.

They knew the risk, though many were new
To the raids by night.
And the enemy fighters took their toll
On courageous crews who flew to hell
On the wings of prayer.
Shot down in flames to burn to death,
Or their loads blown up by foreign fire.

Whilst back at home the wives and mothers
And ops-teams girls would guiltily pray
That the missing planes and those overdue
Would not be the ones of those *they* loved.
And time gnawed by.
But on that night, the waves were alive
As flight after flight
Returned their prayers.
'Our plane's in shreds, but no-one's dead;
On a wing and a prayer, we're coming home.'

***

The twelve-mast clipper
Was Queen of the Seas
In name and fact.
The biggest ship that ever left
Her builder's yards.
Technology edged toward the brink;
So many masts, and sails to catch the wind,
And drive her racing around the globe,
Skimming the crests of the ocean waves,

Risen on foils in mantis prayer.

But on that day a storm surge rose
Where the currents clash,
And Poseidon's daughters spat their rage
And drove the waves to twice the height
Of the twelve-mast Queen.
She lost her masts in a tangled mass
And she rolled three times.

The auto alarm alerted the world,
And heads dropped down
At the terrible loss
Of the gleaming ship and all her crew.
And time gnawed by
Till the radio sparked,
'We're wallowing deep, and praying hard,'
The crackle-voice said. 'The motors work,
And we're gaining her head.
Give us a week, and we'll be in.'

***

The Pride of Rigel's a passenger ship
And a freighter, too.
She's bound for Earth,
But we're filled with dread
For she's long overdue.
She left her home on Planet Steime
On the twenty-third stroke by local time,
And should have been here ten seconds ago.

She *couldn't* be late.

She *had* to appear.
The laws of physics don't allow
For a non-appearance spot on time.
'Space and time can never wait,'
The saying goes.
'Not even a second.'
'Or thirty now,' I check the clocks
And the instruments.

'She's lost,' we say, so empty now,
'For hope is gone.
She's met her fate in the weft of space.'
And time gnaws by.
'Look, look!' A crumpled shape
Before our eyes was forming slow,
Reeling sick in pitch and roll and yaw.

We stand and stare at vision screens
And readouts by the score.
A voice breaks through,
'Captain Greef still in control.
We've aged a year.
Can you get us out?
And Boy! We have a tale to tell.'

CHOICES

'Hey, Erda-man.'

I looked up.

One of the Deanies from the ground crew waved from across the bar. 'Bommy, isn't it?'

'Yes,' I waved back. Some of them like to be seen to know us humans, almost socially. A lot of them call us Erda – it's the humans' long-distant base planet that nobody's ever visited. It's either Erda or Humo, and it's the friendlier of the several generic names for us. I gather there are various uncomplimentary names too, concerning our soft exterior, and rigidity of shape.

'Friend?' one of my companions asked.

'Sort of. It's Prixidd, one of the crew that's coming aboard, to learn the engines, and the decontamination procedures. You must have seen him? That my drink?'

The Slipup Bar on Eighth – it's the second or third one along from the Luridian Cargo entrance – the main ground-to-orbit-shuttle port on Deane. If you don't know the Slipup, it's the same as most other bars close to anywhere with docks. There are always crews and transients looking for a drink and some atmosphere. A bit dim-lit, nothing easily breakable, and an array of seating types to accommodate a variety of body forms. In our case – seats and tables.

There was something of a mix in there – half a dozen fellow Blow-Deck Crew from the Gad Lee May – we're all engine personnel, plus Charz from Clearup. Basically, this lot are my only mates when I'm working. We stick together. Couple of the guys have girls on other planets, but not on Deane – hardly any humans actually live here. Dreary place with sub-zero winter nights and scorching summer days; plus a population that's a bit flexible in body shape. It gets confusing when they change form on a whim.

Plenty of Deanies around the Slipup; most in some kind of port overalls or uniforms. They'll be ground crews, cargo handlers, maintenance crews, securities, customs. Two of them have pilot uniforms on – but that only means they guide a shuttle down from orbit. Amazing to watch them, actually, with two-dozen suddenly-appeared tendrils flashing over the pads.

We don't socialise with them very much. Often work together, yes. But that's limited-speech vocab. So we only share a couple of hundred words, phrases, tonal variations. We're just not natural friends. I suppose the triple arm-set, doubling as tentacles, emphasises the differences.

A few can morph their shapes in imaginative ways; they're a bit like semi-solid jellids. That's extremely useful for the repairsmen, who seem to re-form practically anyhow, depending on the job and the situation, even copy us humans to some degree – like approxy-people.

Some'll do it for fun. Some just for a change: we humans are fairly new to Deane – just a few years, and not too many of us, especially any distance away from the port areas. It's an uninspiring planet, what I've seen of it. I expect they copy our body shapes and mannerisms because we're something different.

'Hey, Bommy. See over there? A couple of Middriggs near the bath-bar?'

'The tall and slenderly sinuous pair? Yes, I see'em – They're attracting a bit of closet attention from the locals. More than us.'

Yes, look at them – silver-skinned silkies in their flowing drapery, lording it in here. Huh, place like this.

'They're slumming it, for the experience on a night out.'

'Probably broken away from their tourist group. Come on, get your drink down you. Let's move on.'

Yes, looking round... a couple more humans the far side. No – four of them, probably dressed-down Bove-Decks crew.

'Might be passengers,' Mirrie wondered. 'I gather we have about sixty this trip.'

'They'll be sealed away from all this. Whisked off to some smart-tart place down the centre.'

'Or stay in one of the In-Port bars, cocooned from the likes of us.'

Seemed like it was human night for the Deanies – a taking-the-pyss night. Not really, I think they sometimes shape-change to make us feel more comfortable – they kinda look up to us cos we go aloft – past-orbit. It's like, we've been *there* – in the Big Vac. They're just awed at the whole concept – can't go themselves – not without full pressure and rad suits. They don't tend to survive a fifty-day trip.

We have a bit of a laugh, josh about this and that; like they snigger and snurg about our sex habits – sex? Habit? *Me?* If only. Our equivalent laugh at them is the way they all go into a fillodian wobble when the moon gets to eclipse the sun – which is a 37-day cycle. So, yes, they get the wobbles more often than I get sex, so let's not go on about it, hmm?

We engaged in tossing an occasional nut across the bar. The edible type of nut, not the screw-it-down kind. I got a well-aimed jolt of squirt joo back from Prixidd. I get on well with him; he's been coming aboard the Gad Lee May with engine parts. We train some of them, including him, in engine maintenance and rebuilding – they love it. Yeah, Prixidd's okay.

'Ay-upper.' Mirrie nudged my elbow, 'Group just come in.' More Deanies, their entry raising a bit of muttering from around the room. But the music was racked up, and I got a whiff of nacrohyte – *Hey, it's gonna be a happy one tonight.*

'Students, they are, all with the compulsory blue collar, shaped in the same way we do.'

'Higher-class than the usual.'

'TerraFed must be the fashion on Deane this year.' We watched them as they went up to the bar, glancing round, trying to look comfortable in a place like that.

'As long as they don't decide on scorpie styles next year. I'm not coming back if they do; the scorpios make my skin itch. Still makes me shiver at the thought of the times I crewed with them, out past Kalèdas and Sigmund.'

The student-looking Deanies were doing the same as the pair of Middriggs, slumming it for thrills, among us port-gutter dross. The port-Deanies nearest us started shuffling, deforming and reforming; muttering about 'Not staying in here with this load of posh-holing...' And were leaving for the Ball Acher's Arms, across the way.

Yipps, the newly-arrived smarty-students had us slummed up. We could hear expressions among them like, 'Dare we?'

'Let's go.'

'Go on, yes.'

They were slinking and sliding into the seats the port-Deanies had just vacated, reforming the seats and themselves, studiously ignoring us – whilst too obviously watching us. Probably remodelling themselves, based on us.

So, without Prixidd and pals, we settled back to the drink, and passed round a few entertain-clips via the eye-chips, Good for a laugh. The new studenty-Deanies were still half-watching us, like studying a tankful of gyppo-fish. Another Deanie I knew – Maxie, I think it was – was talking with one of them. I watched, a bit interested – I've not met many Deanies above the port-and-work status levels. You don't get to be students if you're in the working classes.

Just noticing something that was a bit strange – when the work guys remodel their body shapes on us, they tend to go for an approximation of what they think we look like, and are content with that. Might be the best they can manage, I suppose.

But with this new crowd, it was if they were really studying us; increasingly adjusting to our form, like they've not been near humans before, and wanted to learn.

You could learn from me, I thought. One was definitely forming like a female huma: sleek, with two eyes, eventually. Increasingly resembling a girl I knew some time back – beautiful face. Her body was indefinable, though. I guess even the Deanie students weren't too knowledgeable that way – but the face was sure one I could dream over. *Maybe she's picking my mind,* I half-wondered.

'Y' doing fine,' I tried to encourage that one with a call across to it – not knowing if it was male, female or clomatic. It – she – even managed a very passable smile. And a nod. She raised her glass of Smokey Low in very T-Fed style. I had to laugh – that was the nacro getting to me, as well as her. And I responded the same. Stuffit to Studding Bay – our eyes met! Not possible – they're supposed to be non-functioning when the Deanies mimic the form. But, I felt a kind of kinship – like a touch of a bridge or something.

I took my life and reputation in my backside, and shuffled closer, edging round a bit. My life? – worthless. Reputation? – an ugly bit of an ex-lad? But I was up for it, and asking them, 'You're students? Not seen you in here before? Local, are you? Visiting?'

I find it best to give folk a choice of topics to chat about, without getting to the core, like 'What gender are you? How do you do it? Do you do it? How about it?' And things like that.

Another perfect smile, and she answered in a beautiful accent. *Must be a languages student,* I decided. *That flawless kind of speech style they think is the perfection of our language.* She was pleasant in temperament, too, 'Yes, we are students; having a night out.'

Would never have guessed.

She reached and slid a three-fingered hand round my glass and lifted.

This should be interesting. And drank, eyes sort of asking permission, but not really. She was going to, anyway.

But she sipped, and kept it down, didn't smoke out her new mouth. Another smile, and she slid her drink to me. *Hoooo... could I?* I sniffed at her glass: it was a silicic sullule; the green type. Not a flavour I was fond of. However, in the interest of speci-relations, I took it, raised the glass—

'*Yihhh!*'

A tentack slashed down. Reforming to a gripping fingerhand, tightening round my wrist. A snarling voice. Guttural Terraspeak, sounded forbidding. 'You keep out, Yu*man*.'

Three of them, *Big* Deanies. More like trees than humans or regular port-Deanies, surrounding my new acquaintance, towering round her.

Big Tree-Deanie was pulling at her, pressing her companions away. She was protesting. Resisting. Her friends were forced back by the Biggies. Someone had a farad blade, forearm-long. Tempers suddenly just as sharp. Drinks thrown. One student-type was jerked away. Hurled back. A weird squealing from them. All round – grunting mouths and flashing tentas—

One was gashed open. I was flying back, arm twist-broke by the whirling grip. The others scattering away. She was shriek-fighting.

What is this? Kidnap? Deanap? Murder? Thugs driving them out? Bit brutal. Screeching and yelling increasing in pitch, volume and panic-level. Whole place in pandemonium with all the howling, and stuff flying.

I was sprawled on my back. Right arm agonised. *Shyg! It's been twisted out— Oh, Shyg! That's bad.* My temper asserting itself, I just went at the scrugger who'd done me. Glass shard in my hand as I got up and went for him. He shouldn'a done that to me, for nothing. He wasn't having her: we'd been talking.

Shygle! I was insane with it. The nacrosmoke and drip maybe helped with the intent. Not with the outcome: I was pretty ineffectual, with one arm hanging all twisted and screaming. I got to his neck-thing, slashing with the glass-edge. Shyg, he was tough-skinned. Felt the glass slick into my hand more than his skin.

Tentra slapped round me – waist – left arm. And I was flying, and slamming back down. Blug of a thunk, back of my head. He repeated it, and again. And again. Bastard was doing it on purpose, not even looking. Had three tentacks round me slamming me up and down, and another ripping at me, concentrating on her. She'd lost her humanic look to maybe a sort of doe-cow jelly. Nice-ish.

I couldn't get up – pinned down by his tentacks. He wasn't paying any note of me; just in auto-smashing mode. Could hardly breathe...

She was up; growing taller than him, the thug. Her temper was coming on, too, a reddish tinge round her gill orifices. She snapped at him. Snarled. *Fruggit – they're fighting. Violent arguing, anyway – she ain't going with them – not easily. High pitched, shriek-yells, like a howl. Shyg!* It had the whole place on their tentries, keeping back, watching. All seemingly awed at her defiance. The thuggy trio weren't trying to grab her any more. Chief thuggy was holding back...

Some loud, snapping discussion in Deanie, beyond my working level. different cadences, a whole other language, hardly even similar in tone to the dockies I work with. She was taking charge, turning towards the door, going with them. Her student friends glancing round; one finishing a drink and grabbing a nacro-pot to take out as he chased after them.

Quiet for moments. A murmur starting. The guys trying to get me up, but I was well laid out. Bad breathing – throat really crushed in for a minute or so; and my arm.

'Can't move it. Shygging hurts.'

'Shyg, Bommy, that's bad. Your elbow's out. Rad and ully twist-broke. Shattered, maybe. Shoulder's out. Need to get you A-plus help.'

'Yeah. Yeah. Think y' right.'

'Shyg. Y' head's all splattered at the back, too. Looks bad.'

'Feels it. Gimme a full nacro, back on the ship.'

We were stopped at the inner gates. Not allowed back on board the Gad Lee May. She was undergoing decontamination for a full day, and that meant a day's sealing and preparation beforehand, and a day clear-out and opening-up afterwards.

'We got to get you to a hospital.'

'There isn't one. Not for us humanics.'

'They don't know how to treat us.'

Couple of Deanies were coming round to check on us. Port personnel said they could get me in some place where they might know what to do.

Sure they did. Largely theory of bony endoskeletal beings. Some similarities with their own, semi-skeletal beings with adjustable cartilage internal structures.

I was in there seven days; it took that long to clear up the deep infection that had developed – a common bug found in Deanie claw cuticles. Picked up when Thuggy claw-raked me.

Arm wrecked; they did what they could. Saved it, sort of. My face slashed; one eye not seeing now. Breathing not so good; lung punctured when Thuggy squeezed me.

'At least you're still alive, eh?' As they saw me off and took most of my credits for their trouble.

Couldn't get back aboard the Gad Lee May – it had departed two days previously.

'You?' One of the gatemen checked the records. 'You're down as a deserter. Says here; and I quote, "Did not complete contract. Injured in bar fight. Logged as either deliberate avoidance of contract terms, or wilful refusal to rejoin ship." It's all classed under Desertion. You're therefore down as unreliable, and your head chip has had the programming altered to V4. You won't be able to get aboard any ships. You're blocked.'

His oppo leafed through the regs, 'They've left the rest of the chip intact – you won't be able to kill yourself if you get too pyssed off here.'

'Eh?'

'That's a safety thing on ships – don't want you doing the spectacular suicide-bit in mid-vac, do they?'

'Face it, Bommy. You're marooned on Deane. Killing yourself might have been your best option. And that's out now.'

He was right: I'm stranded. I'm miserable. Can't get back in space. Never get home. All my real mates are on Tay'ath. My family. So few on Deane. Hardly any are resident, and they sure don't want to know the likes of me, how I am now – destitute cripple engine-sumper.

Damn cold in the nights, especially in the gutters. Too hot in the open in the noon sun.

I'm struggling along, cleaning jobs, bars. Sometimes interpret in deals over meals and trips, and disputes over drinks and entry permits.

But this is no life; I am *so* lonely. I'm a sociable guy. I need companionship, especially female, with drinks in hand. This is a desperate life. It's not for me.

I started odd jobs in a couple of new bars, did a few turns as interpreter on short tourist trips for the day-stoppers.

Even saw a couple of ex-colleagues in a bar. They were embarrassed. Left. A few other humans in the bars would only acknowledge me as the local gutterlife, part of the dregs-scene in the dockie bars and fooderies.

Got a one-room pad the size of a crew-cabin. At least it had water and low-C power. In return, I cleaned the front bar every morning – or pm if I had something else on. It was Prixidd's place, and he was okay about my erratic work pattern.

I started to train myself to think of being killed as an okay thing, so my chip won't floor me. It's like re-programming the chip from the inside. So maybe I'll be able to put myself in threat-to-life danger situations. If I think positively about being dead, maybe I can make it happen.

I saw *her* one time. There was this fuss about some biggy Deanie coming round the new transport depot where the tourist trips left from in increasing numbers, apparently. 'Who's she? The tall, undulating female Deanie?'

'Ishmay. The State Governor.'

'She is? She looks like that one who was in the Slipup the night I got done.'

'Could be. There was an attempted coup against her father, and kidnap/assassination of her and her siblings. Father killed, both sibs dead. She succeeded him. Don't know what happened that night, though. Hard to tell: they've been hushy about those times; the family, her guards, or traitor-guards….'

I remember watching her that time at the depot. Remembering how she'd looked – taking on a semblance of that girl I once knew on Tay'ath. Raising her glass; meeting my gaze. Been about to exchange a drink…

Saw her then, coming through, past where we yocky workers were being herded back. Watched her come past. Felt nothing. No emotions either way for her. That girl she reminded me of… yes, maybe.

Not her, though, not Ishmay. She was the elected, appointed, sanctified High Keilsh for the state. Very capable, they said. But what I saw was three pairs of arms like tree-branch tentacles, and teeth to match, in both mouths.

I'd often thought there was more to that group than straightforward students. The colour on her; the height she stretched to. Thuggy got quite deferential when she'd challenged him. Not seeming too certain of his position. Some high family…

More pseudo-shrugging as she and her entourage passed us by, and we were allowed back to the clearing-up tasks they'd assigned us.

So, once I knew, I seemed to notice her more frequently. On the news at one event or another.

Lost my room when Prixidd got a promotion and sold off the front bar. The infection kept breaking out in the deepest of my face slashes, and the medications cost more than I had. Arm was getting worse: it was either dead and useless, or painful as dick-bite and useless. So my work possibilities were becoming somewhat limited. So was food. Drinks nights were a distant memory. Can't get off-planet. Forever on Planet Deane Dump.

She had been my downfall; the instrument of it, if not the perpetrator. Maybe she could be my salvation, too. And maybe the opportunity could be close: there was to be a grand opening of a memorial statue or something, just along the Avenue from the bar where she'd come that night. Memorial to her family and others who'd died in that attempted coup.

Thinking on how they'd been that night, and how she'd looked at the Tourist Depot – all tentacks and teeth, she'd kill me, with the right provocation. No problem. Or her escorts would. All I needed to do was convince my head-chip that I was behaving non-aggressively, until the last nano-second, and then go for her with all three working fingers, and four teeth. Maybe I could blink her to death?

The chance came so quickly and easily. I had no trouble being on the front row where she would parade past for we plebs and workies. It would show she honoured us. In a puggle's arse she did.

Yesss, if I pick my time perfectly, she'll lash back at me, and I'll be mercifully, gratefully dead.

She's coming soon. I see her down the end.

Yes, she'll do it. And that'll be great. Only two escorts, in their high-decorated apparel, and very sharp teeth and hack-blades. Yes, they'll perform the job nicely. And her, in the deepest blue cloak, with silver-steel broad collar. But the throat area is exposed. I'll go for that. I have one half-good arm.

Watching her approach – I'm relaxed. *This will be it... Little does she know... Yeah, one of them will do it, alright. Here... here... coming, closer...* Fingering the edge of my serrascalp. So sharp. I'm getting the head pains that are the total effect of the head chip these days – unless I make any overt attempt to end my own life directly.

Here... here... *Now!*

I duck under the ribbon. Too fast for the lectros, I'm between the escorts – behind her. Slight awareness of shocked frozen faces all around. God – this place is so sterile. Leaping, one forearm flopping round her left shouldine, my blade-carrying right hand at her throat. Poised, half-gripping her, I growl; muttering.

Come on. Come on. Do it. Shygle! Why so slow? You got a death wish? Must be a full second, two seconds, with no reaction from her or her escorts.

She's heaving – her power coming into play. Bending, twin tentas lashing over my back, wrenching me forward, catapulting over, in front of her; practically bouncing to my feet, facing her. *Come on... come on.* I'm half crouching, jabbing at her with the blade. She's towering over me, drawing up to full regal height, tentara flexing, coiling, ready to lash.

Yes... Yes. Come on... come on. Damnit. Come on... kill me.

She flicks a tip – the unutterably useless, non-protective escorts and other port staff still just standing, reactionless. They won't do anything now, not after her forbiddance with that top-flick.

You'll damn do it yourself, then. I'm launching forward, serrascalp leading— *Yurkkk!* I'm throttled to a flying halt by a pair of top tentras as thick as my thigh. *Kill me... kill me.*

She's squeezing, slowly, pulling me in. The near-mouth – those teeth. *Yes, chew me. Rip me to shreds. Get on with it. Sarada! This is bad enough without you playing. Do it.*

She's not going to. Her eyes studying me – glitter-balls, I can see myself reflected in the nearest three. Her teeth retracting. The tentras relaxing slightly.

'I know you, Terrath... Erda. You were there that night. Yagsog pulled you away from me. This is what you do now?'

Kill me... do it.

Her teeth are bared. So long. So sharp. Then retracting again, and she's turning, speaking rapidly to the escorts. Their answers equally as little understood by me. She checks something. Confirms it.

The grip round my throat is easing a fraction. I can breathe. *No, no. Do it, you stupid Keilsh. Tighter, not relaxing, you cretin.*

'Attend to my words. I see who you are. I understand what happened to you. You can continue to struggle, and be very dead in less than a minin. Or. Or we can restore your health and fitness; your face and the dead eye. Your hanging arm. And you can work for me, the State, as liaison with the increasing numbers of humans who are coming here of late. You will have status; rank; and be comfortable. There are females of your species here now.'

Feel bodily good again? comfortable home on Deane? I can't imagine it.

'Decide now, Erda-man.'

Not much of a choice, is it. Here? I'd still be planet-bound on Deane – never travel the Big Black again. Wouldn't ever see my parents again. Won't ever seek out that girl I recall, from wherever.

Her tentacle's tightening a fraction to hasten my choice.

But, with her offer, I'll be able to drink and laugh again with friends in the Slipup and the Ball Acher's. I could be responsible for organising the tourists who regard me now as a bar freak? Be respected. Set up the whole human-Deanie interface. Have a comfortable home, maybe in the Crescents.

Her face softening to look almost humanic... feminine.

'Thanks,' I'm deciding. 'Dead would be good.'

KALEIDOSCOPE

This one is so strange.

At first contact, my breath stills for a moment. I haven't encountered the like before. His mind is a kaleidoscope of jazzing, diamond-like shapes and brilliant colours. They clash and crunch inwards, towards the centre. So very different from anything I've met in all my time doing this. Quite ominous; rather frightening, actually. I shiver.

The mind-pattern changes, losing colour and sharpness. More starkly contrasting, now writhing, like a great mass of snakes, sucking at me.

I shiver again, and cover my disquiet from him, for I am a professional, and do not allow my own feelings to interfere, or to leak.

I call myself a mental artist, a mind sculptor – Miz Zayir, Artist of Glass. What I do is sit with my client – they're all commissions. I don't do them for general sale or galleries. Very close together, we sit, and I put my hands round their head, with our foreheads touching.

I sense into people's minds. I see and feel their aura in my head, and I create a coloured plazglass sculpture to reflect what I've sensed.

But this one... I pause; he's frightening. A jangle of tumbling thoughts that have no shape other than shattered fragments of glass in clashing colours. No. He's back again to squirming, black-and-white snakes, pulling at me.

My normal sculptures are beautiful creations in high-glass. I love them myself. They show how I see my clients, what I sense about them. Some, I remember so well – those I feel most pleased about – a curling figurine, a bird in flight, a sadly drooping flower, a stealthy cat. One was a bright-eyed puppy. Each so individual and precious in exquisite colours and glass, a reflection of the person.

When my sitters come back and I show them my finished work, they say, 'Wow! Awesome. That's just me. It's exactly how I see myself.' They'll press it to their chest, 'I love it. I can so relate to it.' And they hug me and gaze at me in wonder that I had read them so well.

Or puzzling, 'Is that really me?' They know it is, truly, but one or two don't want to see themselves like that. I've only had one who didn't accept it at all. He refused to see any bright interior within himself. And wouldn't pay me; even wanted his deposit back. But that only covered materials, so no chance.

Sometimes, they contact me later, on the phone to tell me how pleased they are, or on my web site with reviews and feedback. And what their friends said.

But how can I do you? I peer within him, and wonder. You're a confusion, so very, utterly different to anything before. *You enshudder me. Do I admit defeat at once and send you away? What's to be frightened of?*

How do I do my artistry? Exactly? I don't know. I see into them, deep, deep down. Into their core, where everyone's insecure and a little afraid – at least a little. But who would want their sculpture to be fashioned to demonstrate that? So I stay with the layer around it and see what sparkles the most down there. They don't want the dark corners, the awful memories... the car crash that was their fault... the lover who spurned them.

I've had the vicious ones and the smarmy ones – men and women alike. I create a sharp-edged crystal or thorny tree for some, a glistening snake, or I even did one like a tornado. I form the sculpture from soft resinous plazglass, with my bare hands and I work non-stop, moulding and shaping and bedding the colour into the material before I bake it in the fire of the oven at 1333 degrees – pleasantly glowing, I tell myself, before allowing it to fine out and slowly cool

But this one. He's different again: one moment a mass of shards with razor edges, sharp shapes that gyrate and tumble, changing, some spiking. Much like the really old toy kaleidoscopes you hold up to the light and twist them to change the display. Then a writhing jangle; a sliding whirlpool. But… But this one had a black background showing through, deepening to the centre.

Dared I glimpse within?

I peeked, and jumped back. A sense of something ravening within, like a rabid dog snarling to get out, to get at me. Yesss… that's exactly what it reminded me of, something ravening deep inside him. I've looked at animals sometimes – my cats and the dog. They were gorgeous, so focused, so complex. I once had a parrot – oh boy – was it mixed-up inside – what scatty little there was. Lovely girl, though.

But this one, he's like an alien, so totally different. His inner being seems somehow so terrible. I daren't let my awareness show. I ease away. Gazing back at him, he's a middle-aged man, smiling, a touch of grey hair, soft hazel eyes – perfectly normal, pleasantly attractive. But, what lurks within. I scarcely breathe. I'm shuddering inside.

'Do you see?' He smiles at me, so softly. 'You do, don't you?'

I scarcely can speak; unable to frame a pleasant, matter-of-fact sentence together to cover for myself.

'Look again.'

He's reaching to me. I feel his grip on my shoulders as we still sit face to face and he's pulling me, insisting, closer to him again. I so nearly wet myself in fear. My eyes close of their own accord, and our foreheads re-touch.

Shock again as I see and feel the jangle jungle there – the covers drawn back. A psychedelic mind hits me at once, all around me in crowding diamonds and needles and spear-head shapes of brilliant, overwhelming colours.

'Be still.' He speaks, perhaps in my head. Is it calming? Or frightening? I can't tell: it's commanding. My heart seems to sink, become empty. I'm fighting the stabbing shards in my mind, so afraid. Is this how it is for some of the people I do this with? They've never said.

'Be still,' he says again. My eyes open. His are barely an inch before me. Almond eyes framed in dark lashes. A pale, streaked blue iris around a black pupil that seems to draw me in. I resist, but I'm not moving. I close my eyes to shut out his black pits. The kaleidoscope is there again, restless, shifting, as though crawling over me.

I shudder.

'Be still,' he repeats. *'See.'*

Among the tangled mass of shifting bright shards, the middle ones are fading, taking a different form, smoother again, twisting like fingers wringing…

'See.'

Afraid, I feel his hands tighten around my head as he keeps me close, and I watch the scene forming within my closed eyes. The centre of my kaleidoscopic jangle is becoming an opening, a pathway. With tall trees around, enclosing it, bathed in the warm medley of autumnal colours. A tunnel-like track, carpeted with golden leaves, leading – I looked ahead – into brightness. I was being pulled in. Into increasing brightness.

'No. No.' I resist.

But he holds me firm. 'Come home, *mi Priya*.'

I realise. I know now. I see, remember. He is Khairt! My one-time partner. Our home was there. Along the wooded pathway. My home of wonder and comfort. The home I fled these ten years since.

'You've been lost.'

'No, I'm not lost. Not at all. I've been here. This planet has a raw beauty, *mi Khairt*. This Earth. I have happiness here; challenge and inspiration.'

'Come back with me.' His voice and hands urge me. Pulling at me to reinforce his command.

'No.' I resist more strongly. 'You've come. You've reminded me of other times and places, that I want not to revisit. I have cleared my mind of all my past – of you… of that home. You are forgotten to me. This Earth is now my—'

'No. *Mi Priya*. Return with me.' He insists; becoming stronger. 'To your home.'

If only he'd beseeched, implored. But no, not *mi Khairt*. That was never his way. 'It's always the order, the impellent, with you, isn't it?'

'But your home—'

I broke away, 'My home? Is here now.' His eyes, now so blue and softly-seeing. Not his normal self – the hard angles and sharp jangles of the kaleidoscope; the embodiment of authority. Trying the oiled-python approach now

You come here, to my new home. Hiding behind the gentle greenery of your guise. Your idea of an enticement, perhaps? But I saw the sharpness at once, the angles, the hard edges that personify you. I just hadn't recognised you in human form beneath them.

He stares, deep and hard into me, willing me to capitulate, to surrender to him.

I stare back, my implacability strengthening.

You have no power over me now I know you.

Slowly, we separate as he releases my head.

'I could—'

'I know you could, *mi Cinta Lama*. But if you were to harm this planet – my refuge – in any way, I would so utterly extinguish you and all else that you hold dear.'

He stares back into my depths, undecided. I see his turmoil – the threats and violence – the very reasons I left him. I see the cruelty there; the lurking direness that would await me should I return with him. He's summoning up the best tactic… the fastest attack. But is shrouded with doubts. Is he not so totally committed, now that he has found me?

A second thought?

I pre-empt any further protest, anger or action he might summon up. 'Believe me,' I tell him, 'I would completely destroy and life you have. Your friends and family, I would ruin. You would have nothing. *Be* nothing.'

I wait. *Is he taking further thought on the matter?*

'Let us call it quits at this,' I say again. 'Say you never found me – as indeed you haven't, and never will

– I'm not that person now, and never will be again. You lost me then, not now.'

Again, he stares, but he's looking for his way out now, not challenging. Somewhere among the wriggling kaleidoscopic worms and splinters, he must have found it. He nods. 'So be it.' And I know he truly accepts it.

'So be it,' I echo.

Silently now, he stands and leaves, fading as he nears the door to my studio.

I sit back, my mind awhirl. Soon to be calm again when I re-close the memories. I'll permit myself a few minutes of reverie of those dark, biting times on Skrakk, and then it will be gone forever.

I shall see my lover tonight, Michael Silversmith – by name and occupation. It is not unfeasible that he might propose to me again, for my demeanour will encourage it.

Perchance, this time, I shall accept.

JUST SOME OLD GUY

I collected my pension at the bank, paid my two regular bills for this month, and was heading – tottering, more like – to the pub to see my mates and have my afternoon drink in Wetherspoons.

Hardly got a hundred yards, just round the corner onto Wellington Street, and this youth's coming at me fists first, knocking me flat back. I'm rolling over in a tangled, shocked-to-death heap all legs and arms flying and head on the pavement and he's on top of me and hitting my face and snarling like he's got rabies and mauling at me and hitting me and he's got my money; and still kicking and snarling and ranting. And he's going and running off and he's laughing.

'I got a view of him,' I told the police, and described him very clearly, right down to the wart on the side of his chin and the scrubby little moustache on his ferrety face.

'They weren't interested. *Not interested!*' I told my mates. They were full of sympathy and bought me an extra half. 'But that policeman told me I had no visible injuries, so I should go to victim support. Huh. No help at all.

'I told him I just gave him a very clear description. But he said I couldn't see a thing. You know, got that touch of derision, how they do.

'I could then, I said. A bit blurred now cuz I hit my head. That kid hit my head, too.

'But the officer said again I wasn't visibly harmed; so get myself to A&E if I was worried. "Otherwise, this is an incident, not a crime." He put on his special ponderous-idiot voice for that bit, and shrugged when he read out the incident number to me. He even expected me to write it down myself.

'I didn't know what to do with that number. Asked him if I should I phone it, or re-program the combination on the door?

He shrugged again and spoke with his gormy-looking over-scrubbed oppo with the Brylcreem hair. I heard him saying, "Nah. Just some old guy, witter-arsing away."

He looked over my head, and nodded to somebody queuing behind me, dismissing me. Ignorant git.

So I concentrated on getting well. It wasn't easy. I was really shocked by the whole occurrence. I mean, at my age, getting knocked over on the pavement is not helpful to my well-being. Especially so close to home, where I always felt safe before.

Well, anyway, after a time, I was getting on a bit better and had a sub from Victim Support, and carried on with my little job caretaking and cleaning round the flats – all the concourses, picking litter and sometimes hosing down, depending what filthy vomiting, peeing or defecating party somebody had had the night before on the landings.

Hello – that's him.

Three floors below, in the quad where the garden benches are. I'd know that figure, and hoodie, anywhere. He was yelling into some old lady's face and she was answering him back and he hit her and was ripping her bag away and went dashing off.

'He's coming up this way.' Obvious escape route – up to this floor, where the main landings go from one block of flats to the neighbouring ones, and he can make his escape in any of four directions.

Up here, it's concrete steps. Bare brick and concrete walls. Scaffold pipe hand-railings. Cigarette ends in a cluster; couple of packets'-worth. He'll be bouncing up this way, two at a time, not looking, just gloating.

I wasn't going anywhere. I waited. Perhaps twenty... thirty seconds. Here, he's close... *Now!* He rounded the corner straight into my fist.

It took his face apart. Nose disintegrated – splattered apart. Blood everywhere, and he went flying back down the steps – feet flailing. Tumbling in a crumpled heap on the next landing.

I only permitted myself a small smile, for around three seconds, then went back to my own flat to get changed – there was so much blood splattered all down me.

The police came round that evening, canvassing for witnesses. They were concerned about the youth.

'You weren't bothered about him before,' I said. 'When he was a clear and present danger to the community.'

'He's a hospital case,' my previously unconcerned officer lamented, when he'd finished giving me a funny look. 'Like an iron fist went through his face.'

Totally destroyed his looks,' Lady officer with sad eyes and dark roots said. 'Cheek and jaw bones broken. Teeth... One eye.'

'They don't know if he'll ever recover.'

'We can but hope,' I said. 'He had a terrible appearance when he came at me the other week; I don't imagine it can be any worse. Besides, as you told me previously, officer, there's hardly anyone round here to witness anything, day or night. I expect it was him, frightened everybody off.' I can look and sound everso innocent.

When they'd gone, I felt quite pleased, looking at my right fist. I allowed it to morph into its natural form, a shellac claw. Big, solid and strong enough to smash through concrete, so a human face was scarcely noticeable. I flexed it a little. Smiled. Keeping up this senile human image is pretty good for the disguise angle, but it's so satisfying to resume my native form now and again. You know, stretch all my legs at once; unfurl my eye stalks to their fullest extent; rattle my tail plates…

Oh, yesss. I'll enjoy a drink of putreen for relaxation. Then I'll get back to my real caretaking job – taking care of my next incoming group of colonists from the orbiting transfer station, ready to take up their so-well-disguised role among the general Earth population.

We don't want any further delay to our little occupation schedule, do we?

THE EMPEROR'S NEW CLOTHES

> Emperor Semokken.
> Born: 4040? OC Time.
> Reign: 4060? to Unknown; possibly continuing.

Source: PaedioGalaxia.
Reference: Outline History of the Central Orion-Cygnus Empire.

Dates are tentatively included as estimates, partly because of lack of certainty, but also because it is generally considered to be unwise to publicly speculate about the person of absolute power within an empire. This is particularly relevant here, in view of innumerable rumours that the Emperor Semokken may or may not be the same actual personage throughout this extended period – it being well over one hundred years since 4060, OC Time.

The PaedioGalaxia includes a further entry:

> Around the years 5000 to 5005, after 40+ years as ruling *mitre*, it was believed by some that the emperor's health was failing. There was no indication of this, however, in the public eye, as the emperor was seen on General Issue Broadcasts as almost-daily news items. His live public appearances were as erratic as ever, and, as always, largely dependent on which major events he attended on various planets.

The possibility that any or all of these 'casts and personal appearances may have been made by a stand-in is frequently whispered, as is the likelihood of pre-recorded, re-mastered showings. But this is always so when powerful people make personal appearances of any kind. It demonstrates, as often as not, that the ruler governs with guile as well as power; especially when he or she is considered to be at any risk of assassination.

Seemingly, the emperor's health abruptly improved, and his public appearances increased in frequency and stellographic range.

Recently, a collection of documents, pods, casts, vids and stillics has come to light, following the expiry of the hundred years rule on such state-related data. The following account cannot be verified, but there is no specific reason to doubt its validity, particularly as it fits with numerous known facts, and anecdotes of the time, many suppositions, and the guaranteed origin of the package, still in official Imperial State seals.

Viz:

Late-eight shift, and we were unexpectedly relieved of duties.

'Other matters,' some real high official told us. 'We're taking over hospitality. Go home.'

Going home is difficult when the orbit-to-ground shuttles are full this time of day, and my ticket is for seven hours' time. So we were chatting on about the weather on Zilth, and on Makris. And the lack of heating controls up here on Transit Orbital Station 2A. Plus the Spikes Game yesterday. And Zippy's daughters – every one a little jewel. And my wife, Odyssa, a somewhat larger jewel, but such a treasure.

It was the usual low-level drink-fuelled chatter when you're hanging around waiting for a connection or for someone to turn up, or, in our case, when you've been given the evening off at short notice and can't get home till the rush is done. You know, idle chit-chat with a mate in the waiting lounge when you're too tired to bother, really.

It's not like the Second Class OT Waiting Lounge on Orbital 2A is anything special – all ultrene leather and sateen steel, gleaming mirrors and loosely be-smocked waiters. But it was the only place to sit ourselves down, even if we staff weren't normally allowed to drink in there. The view through the panorama-screens at the time was mostly stars and a few parked up interstellar ships. With the spin, it'd drift over the night side of Zilth within the hour.

'Yipps, Max, you fell on y' feet with her, eh, your Odyssa? Sweet tempered is she? like sweet-bodied?'

'Don't be crude about my dearly beloved, Zippy,' I told him. I really meant that; I always do, especially when I've had a drink.

So Zippy changed the subject. 'I hear Emperor Semokken is coming to Zilth. Might be coming here, through Trans Orbital 2A.'

'Reckon that's why we've been laid off for the duration?'

'Bet he's got some conference or planet-opening event to show his face at. Or execute a few dozen government officials, maybe.'

'Mmm,' I knew what he meant. 'Our lot have been mouthing off about imperial matters more than they should.'

'It'll probably just be one of his gang of substitutes and lookalikes. Hardly something to get excited about, is it?'

'Yeah, it is.' I was up for it on the excitement level. 'To be on the same orbit station as *The Galactic Emperor?* Yes, that's something, alright. It is to me. I'm getting an awesome sort of feeling at being anywhere near his presence. Like – I'm on the same station as *Emperor Semoken*. It's—'

'Yeah, we know, *awesome.*'

'Sure; I know he's not really *Galactic* Emperor—'

'Merely a title,' Zippy butts in again. 'Galactic Vanity, more like. Emperor of less than a millionth of the galaxy – 189 planets plus 300-odd independent and colonial moons and planetoids, asteroids and one long-cycle comet.' Zippy could be a tad disparaging about authority figures when the mood took him.

'Nearly five hundred? That's still pretty good – I mean, he's *the* top guy in the whole empire. One rung below *The Almighty*. Absolute power, he is. And he's coming *here? Wow.*' Perhaps he's actually here; within breathing-the-same-air distance. I mean – that's just Yoiks!'

'He'll only be passing through – probably here already. It's got to be his security team that's been pestering round the transit lounges, kitchens, conference halls, stopover berthings, repair shops, storage and retai—'

'Yeah yeah,' I stopped him going on with the whole audit. 'We know all the bits of our own orbital station – you don't have to catalogue them. What's he doing here, though? Must be a reason to come to our little neck of the cluster.'

'Something highly clandestine and deviant; having an affair, I bet.'

'More likely a vengeance check-over. He likes the personal touch when he's sanctioned a few disposals.' That's what I hear, anyway.'

'Maybe a one-to-oner with Chairman Xond – I heard a rumour he was here.'

'What? Xond? Of the Xanbers?'

'Yeah – rumour is, they're wanting to join the Empire, but the emperor's got a personal grudge against them, and is blocking it.'

There he goes – Zippy on the negatives again.

'Excuse me, gentlemen.'

Sassa! That made me jump – never saw anyone sneaking up on us.

'May I join you in the drinks – My round?'

I turned and looked up. Some guy with metallic silver-gold hair. I'd seen him earlier, pre-checking everyone in the lounge. All plaz-suited up, studying everybody and everything, whether or not it moved.

'Er, we're actually not supposed to be drinking in this lounge,' I apologised. 'We're staff from the other lounge; the VIP hospitality quarters. Tossed out for the remainder of the shift.'

'Yeah, we wondered who'd invaded us; kicked us out for the evening,' Zippy let him know about his displeasure. 'Then we decided it's got to be the emperor come to see us; and you must be one of the Imperial Party, sussing the place out.'

'T'is the emperor, is it? Brings all his own staff, I expect? Including you, eh?'

Plaz-suit-and-metallic-hair gave us the total dead-eye. Obviously didn't like such things being spoken aloud. 'I'm looking for someone to do a small job for us this evening. Well-paid, food thrown in – or carried in very carefully, actually.' He stared at me.

'How well paid?' Zippy is the money guy on every occasion.

'What is the job?' I liked the sound of food that wasn't the packeted and tepid junk they serve in the OK Lounge. And if it was in the VIP lounge where I usually worked, I knew what might be on offer to top-echelon folk. And they don't come any more top-ech than *The Emperor.*

'Someone to join us at the emperor's table – we need an extra person; someone's unavailable; we don't like empty seats.'

Now, I'm not stupid – well, I am, but not *that* stupid, or I wouldn'a made sub-super in the VIP hospitality lounge. Although I put my success down to a pleasant personality more than brains.

'There has to be more to it than that.' I looked pointedly at him, still awaiting the drinks he'd mentioned. 'You could take a chair away.'

'No, no. All above board. Someone can't get, indisposed. We need an even number. You'd sit in the company of some very important people.' He was focusing on me. 'You'd be about right, body and features-wise.'

Even I wasn't going to fall for that. 'You mean a few of the party have chicked out, and you want a few locals to make up the numbers? Did they decide they had a more important meeting than having a super-posh meal that lasts four hours? And probably ends on the gibbet? Or they've heard about some bomb plot or other?'

'They'll either,' Zippy was getting into the swing of this, 'be shagging the shell off one of the outworlders we meet round here' – not that they really got shelly carapaces, y'understand, but they get that shelly sheen on their skin – 'or a discussion on high-level Empire business with someone who's officially not on Transorb 2A. Maybe some rebel group surrendering somewhere?'

I think Plaz-suit decided Zippy definitely wouldn't be the one to take into some official function with that mouth on overtime. And Zippy was hot-dating with some through-passer from Endice. So he wasn't going to miss a chance like that, not for the sort of meal we ladled out every next day. He didn't know about the two thou creds I was offered on the way out. For four hours' work sitting at a table. With decent food and drink actually presented to me.

So, I went with Supersmart Guy in the lectro-blue plaz-suit, and there was a man and a woman in the inner sanctum where we usually play cards when we're off-duty.

I know you from the telebi, I thought. *You're the emperor's wife – Lady Empress – arm-hanger, whatever.* She never speaks. She's never introduced or mentioned. She's a *viz*-aid, not audio support. *He's* The Man.

But he ain't here. And they're holding these semi-uniform cream jackets up next to me for a good fit. You know, like *Imperial* Cream. Can't stand it myself; looks like soymilk gone off.

But I'm like utterly awed – she's *The Empress*. Like Mrs God. It came over me. All open-mouthed and frozen at the sight and the thought of the highest woman in the whole empire. I was trying the jacket on – The Imperial jacket! Like – *his*. His mighty Emperorship! Even if it was a shit style – up to its neck in medals and braid. So what the chuffaluff's going on here?

They were fiddling with it, pulling and tugging at me. Bit of tweaking going on, too. And I'm watching her Empressness, and she came at me, and leaned in, and spoke. She whispered something to me. But Yipps – her accent: I didn't understand a word.

I don't pudding around once I get started on a job: I mix it in. Yes – if there's talking to be done, I'm your man. So I came up with some total witticism, of course, cos I'm like that. Something like, 'These jackets'll have to go.'

She kept shushing me while I was being dressed – and it was like they thought I didn't recognise the Emperor's iconic rigout. Not my style at all, but I already told them that. 'I prefer the smocks our waiters wear – change colour with the light,'

So I'm to be sitting at a banquet table, pretending to be Emperor Semoken, and waited on hand and fart by a horde of simpering Yakoes and Servies. If any of them is from our in-Orb staff, they'll know me the instant they see my jewel-like face. Unless… they're doing make-up on me, and saying, 'You look a bit like him, anyway.'

'If I shut my eyes…'

'You have a similar build.'

'This'll disguise you enough.'

'Most of the staff are our own entourage,' says Metal Head, 'so nobody'll dare to look too carefully. Besides, they're used to having a different-looking emperor every meal; what with the stand-ins. Don't even notice – it's the clothes and regalia they serve, not the person's face.'

I mentioned they'd need to become more versatile if I ever became emperor. 'I'd wear something different every day, so they had to look more closely. Starting with something humble, but smart – like the waiters in here.'

Yeah, I can live with pampering for an evening – while Semoken gets up to whatever with his high-power discussions or deep-power screwing. As long as this isn't because they've caught wind of some assassination plot for tonight. I resolved to be careful who was sidling up close to me. Or pointing anything other than a spoon at me. And there's the cash-inducement, too. Odyssa will be super-chuffed about an extra cash-inflow just as the spending season begins.

So half an hour later, I'm sitting there, eating all this gorgeous stuff, which was okay by me. And chatting and drinking with all these guests and visitors and really top-posh folk. Resisting all the aides' mild efforts to stop me doing both. But their efforts were in vain: I like imbibing and talking. And when one's free and I'm the emperor, they didn't stand much chance of stopping me.

Yeah, yeah, I know. You'd think nobody was going to be fooled by me being the Big Man, but, as Silver Head explained, 'See all these telebi units all around? They're empire-run and we have live-active image-manipulation like you never saw, so you'll look exactly like Emperor Semoken when it goes out – five min delay.' The way they said delay – like dee-lay – made me laugh; and confirmed they were real and it was serious.

It started off as a great night. Totally mongreled out, I was, in record time; drinking hooch like that. I mean, the price was in orbit. I know, I'm usually serving it out to the garland brigade. Who with any sense of justice, is going to turn that down? Not me, for sure. And me practically running the show – bet they never had a subsi-emperor as loquacious as I am before. I mean, they got to have some stand-in every time the emperor fancies getting his end away, playing with his shell collection, meeting an ambassador, cutting a few throats, watching The Game or whatever. Suits me.

I was the wow of the night. I could tell from the looks on all their faces – the guests were all delighted by my galvanic wit and my occasional sly dig at some toadrag in the Empire I heard of, or I'd seen snarking up on the telebi. My aides and things pretended to be horrified, or a few were amused, I suppose.

Course, Mrs Empress – Aimee – or Ayer-mee – as she kept saying, was right next to me, and we exchanged dialogue between mouthfuls. I told her, 'You'd be a lot better off if you were called Zykon. More power to a name like that. Like Semoken – that's the ultimate name for a man. Zykon would go well with it.'

She actually laughed and said, 'Flyke off, you twad. You're here for the evening – not a millisecond longer.' I could tell she was already regretting my impending departure, but *Cellar V*.

Yeah, okay – bearing that exact fact in mind – that my departure would be any sec now, I was going to make the most of it – the two thou creds were in my account and non-refundable. And the drinks I've necked back must have cost about the same, and they sure aren't refundable. Plus a couple of monogrammed Imperial souvenirs off the table into my inside pocket.

Naturally, the Empress was very keen to talk with a new emperor like me. 'Makes a refreshing change, I imagine?' I said.

'Certainly different,' she huffed. 'Having you here is like having to wear a peasant's straw underwear for an evening.'

But we got on great, really. I saw her shake her head a few times, and I said, 'Wait till I get you in bed – this's nothing.' She actually laughed at that. It was the same sort of laugh as Grim Reaper has on Death Abounds on the telebi.

'Four hours,' she said. 'Not one second longer, then you're back in the cess whence you came.'

'Language like that – from the First Galaxia! You should be ashamed,' I said. 'The language I've heard round here tonight, my Odyssa would be shocked.'

The entertainment was appalling, naturally. 'The emperor must have dreadful taste in jokes,' I told'em, when the laugh-liners were on. 'And magic acts.' *Magic acts*, of all things.

'They're going to have to stop when I'm in charge,' I thought I might as well go out on a high, as my time was nearing the chime.

People were coming and going; not just the servers, there were messengers, too. Bringing little lectro-screens to me with stuff on them – all sorts of writing and glyphs and data.

'The Emp must be awful busy,' I told one of the aides. 'No wonder he needs nights off.' But it was just so it would make him look as if he was earning his keep. Talk about incomprehensible – all these messages on little screens. But after the first few I dropped one into the soup tureen. They stopped bringing them after that.

'No point even pretending with this guy,' one said.

Things went better after that, for perhaps an hour, with some different drinks, a variety of snacks, a really decent singer lady who came and sat with us for a time and was really nice. There was a few degrees thaw from Mrs Emperor after that; I think she was jealous of the attention I paid to The Voice of Angelicus. We actually managed to laugh at a couple of jokes we each told, and a couple of You'd-never-believe-it stories about people we'd come across in our respective roles as Sub-Manager of the hospitality suite, and Empress Galaxia. Whole new realms of experience for both of us, I imagine

In the middle of all this revelry and imperial play-pitting, I noticed three of the upper strata on our table were conferring together, and nodding to me and Aimee before they upped and left. *Some minor imperial inconveniency,* I decided. *Empy's decided to bonk a dawgler or something of the sort, while he's here and got the chance.*

So I tried one of the hilkini prawns that does this pseudo-twitching when you bite it. Absolute flood of flavour then. Now that was real magic – never had one before. Aimee had supped more than her usual quota, I imagine, and she was really Ayer-mee-ing it up. *You're not too crappy when you're liquidised,* I was thinking, and had a couple more palpitating prawns.

One of the recent departees returned, looking bothered. He went round whispering to some of the other aide-types, and looking kinda grave.

So. I'm the Emperor at the Table, and thus in charge. I asked a couple of them. They ignored me, so I stood up and said really loudly, 'I am The Emperor Semoken. So tell me.' I was conscious of the telebi suddenly focusing tight on me. I never saw the real emperor do that. *I bet they delay this bit and edit it out.*

A couple of them – both ladies, and truly classy with it – came over and sorta mentally stroked me. 'There's been an accident…'

'Could you keep going a little longer until it's sorted? I'll stay with you, while the Lady Imperàta goes with my colleague.'

I did a lot of compliant smiling and said I'd stay as long as they kept stroking and paying. One sat with me. To keep me under control, I suspected, so I tried it on and stroked her leg.

She didn't like it, of course, but she smiled and whispered, 'I'll rip your eyes out if you carry on doing that, telebi or not.'

'I don't need eyes when my tactile senses are so well-tuned to your presence,' I replied, with not a break in the rhythm or bones of my fingers.

I could tell that she tried not to smile as she bent my fingers back under the table and I said, 'You wouldn't do that if I was the real emperor.'

She said the real one wouldn't do things like that to his daughter. That sank in, and I let go – like she was my daughter, too. But I thought, *I bet you ain't his daughter, and I'm not him,* and put my hand back and said, 'Smile for the telebi.'

So they had me stay for the after-dining chat in another room I never been near before. It was as though they'd brought it with'em and fitted it in, complete all these super-posh folk – ladies *and* men. Some I recognised from local politics and business, and meetings up here on Orbit 2A on occasion. Seen'em on the local telebi, too. Yes, a recent 'cast was about a group of near-group planet traders, as I recall.

It settled again, and all the loose folk came to rub noses with the Galactic Emperor – *Me!* I was really popular – being so approachable when I'm pastied, and I was insisting I go round and shake hands, bow and fingertip noses. I did a couple of high-tens, but I had to put my drink down to do it, and one of my so-called aides swiped it every time.

'Get your own drinks,' I told him. 'Filch mine once more, and you're fired.'

So I wasn't putting my drink down again after the last one vanished and I had to nick some other cunny's who wasn't holding on to it tightly enough.

I did the chatting and laughing and knew more jokes than the rest put together. They had to laugh, anyway, me being the emperor, with a bit of a reputation for people-disposal. Couple of self-handshakes – I think that had something to do with wishing someone happy masturbation. Nose-rubbing, cheek-m'wahing and tongue-sticking were popular, too.

Apparently, Real Empy is a fuddering old docker when it comes to things like getting up close, greetings and won't even touch knucks on the odd occasion he bothers to get up, or speak to anyone. So today's emperor is a bit of an eye-opener, as well as lady-tickler if you turn your back. I'm sure some of them noticed the change, but no-one said anything. Not to me, anyway.

In the midst of all this revelry and jolly-making, I did a few deals that sounded okay to me – like about granting public access to the Imperial Forests on Zilth… and dropping the Imperial import/export tax by fifty-percent. I mean – this is my home planet, too. Got to look after it.

All these local Bigs were delighted with the sudden agreement on some totally important planetary matter. I also kept seeing these ultra-urgent looks on some faces and super-dramatic whisper-asides. I didn't even have to figure there was something serious going on behind the scenes I was creating – it was moldifyingly obvious. Funny, that, stitching people and deals up, however I felt like doing.

So, getting away with the first few, I thought I'd do one or two more, while I was there, and asked some local guys I often saw on the telebi what they'd really like from this Imperial visit.

So we did that as well.

Then, a silver-edge-suited top-aide came whispering that I was needed a little longer. Great, I thought, a few more deals, and I can wangle myself into being over-manager of the hospitality suite, permanent. With a raise and pension, courtesy of the emperor himself.

'Somebody shot The Emperor, have they?' I ear-grabbed Silver-tips a bit later, when it was going on way past the time they'd said. He went slightly grey-green, as well as red.

'It's kin obvious,' I said, 'the way you're all squirking round. How much are you paying me for overtime?'

So I stayed up nearly all night, and it turned out Emperor Semoken had been meeting with Chairman Xond, of the Xanbers Union about admission to the Fed.

'The discussion with Chairman Xond became somewhat heated, and the emperor, er, had a heart attack. While the docs were treating him in the clinic unit, there was, er, an explosion in the discussions suite.

The whole room de-aired. Three of our senior staff and four of theirs are dead, including Chairman Xond. Four bodies are in pieces, drifting low, wide and descending to re-entry.

'So you must stay on as emperor until we sort it all out.'

And I said, '*You* don't order The Emperor round.' *I got to get into role, you know, if it's going to continue till they get it organised. It could take days – at two thou credits per four hours. Fuckerty-foo – I'm practically rich if this carries on till the deccend. Wait till I tell Odyssa about this.* 'You have to say "Please" if you want something, even from the Temp Emp.'

So I started emperoring it round even more and asking on the quiet what was happening about the Galactic Big Guy.

And they said, 'Er, that's the awkward bit.'

'But he's okay? Brought round? Resting?'

'Heart ruptured open. Brain starved too long. Dead as a dondon's ding-dong. Er, not to put too fine a point on it.'

'So?' This left me in something of a pickle – I'd already missed a couple of shuttles back home. 'My Ody'll be worrying.'

'We can let her know you've been delayed. You're going to have to carry on here for a time – Emperor Semoken had several other engagements to attend in the immediate future.'

'Important ones?'

'They're all important if The Galactic Emperor is there.'

I gave him my funny look, 'And your other substitutes aren't here?'

He pulled a face like a sluggle's anal orifice.

'So who's next on the Big List of Succession?'

Another face-pull, but he didn't say anything.

'What about Ayer-meee?'

Another twisty face and no answer. 'We merely need you to cover for a few days while we make the arrangements. *Please.*'

I decided. 'Tell my Odyssa I'll be late home; and to keep checking the bank account. I'll have a chat with the Xanbers, hmm?'

And I did. Eight of them in a side-suite, kinda worried in case they were blamed for whatever had happened – like bumping the emperor off, blowing themselves up, and eating fishcakes before the main course.

'The emperor?' I said. 'Don't fret yourselves about him,' I told them. 'I lose substitutes now and again… and again. He wasn't a very good one – got too carried away with it sometimes.'

They felt better after that, and I further raised their spirits by asking them to explain again about the matter they'd been discussing. They did – all about having the right to be admitted to the Empire as Full Independents, not as a vassal planet of some other crappy planet where they do that appalling sudsy real-life vomit-inducer programme – Erastend. Had to agree with them there: the Erastenders on the vids looked utterly moronic. Who'd want to be ruled by them?

So the upshot was I agreed with their petition to be free of their supposed masters. We got the telebi in and rubbed genitals – no, we didn't – I was joking there;

they're hand-shakers. Although I did offer, with Miss Xond the Younger.

So anyway, my Aide-lot said they'd get it all sorted with my Ody, and, 'No, you can't write or vid to tell her you're going to be The Emperor for a few days – it's a secret. We'll handle it discreetly.'

'Er, meantime, you're due on Makris tomorrow.'

'Busy schedule.'

'The ship has to leave at dawn, Central-Zilth time.'

It's amazing what they can do with makeup, and hint-stories and the telebi manipulations, and public memory. They screw the old vids about so much, you can't trust your own recollection of what the Emperor Galactica looked like a dozen days ago. Youks – I don't trust my own memory of what *I* looked like a dozen days back. I bet they can change what you see in mirrors, too.

But anyway, it's not all bad, being the Emperor Galactica. There's the massive banquets; and travel; and meeting hundreds of planetary top-bods that I have to tolerate, or not; plus vat upon vat of the most divine drinks; and some women seem to throw themselves at me.

'Are you paid to do this?' I asked one. And the emperor got his face slapped! So I take'em at face value now – or tit-value, mostly. And there's all the chatting and laughing and drinking and improving Imperial relations. Seems I'm doing okay there. Nobody's suggested I step down, mentioned an impending heart attack for me; left a bomb lying round; or pointed anything at me.

I'm doing okay with Empressa Ayer-mee as well. Not that we do anything untoward. We don't... you know.

We have a sort of sharing arrangement. She has her friends and I have mine. She's totally in the background with all her ladyfriends, so I don't have to put up with her sarkiness all the time. I thought I might phase her out before long.

So, basically, over the past year, it seems to be working well. Empire GDP – that's what they call the economy – is at record levels. Trade and wealth abound; and the contentment index is way beyond – judging by me, cos I'm sure happy enough. My pack of entouragers is as well: I don't do silly demands on them, and I cut down on the number – around two hundred down to two dozen really nice ones. The 195 full planetary members of the Empire seem happier than they had been for a while, and nobody's mentioned I seem different. Maybe scared to – in case I change back, or change my mind on some recent decisions.

So I'm optimistic that Odyssa will be understanding, kind, and really forgiving when I get back to Transorb 2A next decca. Hopefully, she'll join me as Mrs Emperor.

I'm quite looking forward to the next hundred years or so.

Several observations are perhaps worth making at this point:
The empire has more than doubled in size since the year 5000.
There have been no wars or rebellions since 5015.
Interplanetary trade has multiplied by a factor of twenty in overall volume and value over the same period.
The Empress Odyssa appears to be the same actual person who was first noted in 5005, although, of course, appearances are no guarantee of anything.

Emperor Semoken has veered away from the Regal Cream uniform that was, for at least a thousand years previously, worn by the Imperial Personage. It has been supplanted by pdp – photo-dichroic-pastels – which change colour subtly, as the light catches them. It is thought that this is an acknowledgement of the multiple colours of the many peoples and species who harmoniously populate the New Galactic Empire. Similarly, the style of his attire is no longer of a military nature: it is more in the mode of the loose tunic of lowly waiters, or servers, signifying, the emperor says, that it is he who serves the people.

The emperor's new clothes do indeed symbolise his reign as one of peace, increasing prosperity, and subtle change.

A BIT OF BOTHER

The emergency klaxons were nearly blasting the Pride of Otton apart. I was off my null-g bed in a flustered, panicking second. 'What the hedreth is that?' I'm ranting as I'm getting my stuff on. Suckit – no bra to hand.

'You mean, what is it, *exactly?* No idea,' says Hosky-my-bunkie. 'Just a bit of bother, I expect. Emergency of some sort.'

'This ship's always in some sort of bother.'

'Never heard that tone before.'

'Nor me. Get to the Point Station. Fast.'

I was panicking fractionally less as I dressed, or dragged and forced things on, and we didn't get vapourised.

'So it can't be streme bad,' said Hosky, on his way out and I'm following him down the corridor. 'Grav's still on. We still got power.'

We get to the Point Station and there's around a thousand other crew milling round the big yellow signs and the UV lights. Okay, so there was maybe two dozen crew, but it sure seemed like a trillith or two.

'A section of the outer hull, amidships, has suffered a catastrophic crack,' the senior mate was saying. 'That's what I've been told. I don't know how big *catastrophic* is, but the captain sounded flustered when he first briefed us. Then we got the signal that the split was spreading and could lead to a major rupture of the inner skin.'

'So it *is* a streme mergency?' says Hosky, looking worried as the Whittling Whistler.

Senior Mate Refdene looked a touch frantic himself, and kept cocking his head. *Must be listening in to ongoing updates.*

'We all need to get into light duty vac-suits,' he suddenly tells us, 'and make our way to the lifeboat points.'

'Shuffles! Hosky? Hosky! Where you gone?' The bottle-nosed buggra had gone. Vanished down the corridor. Front of the queue, he was. So much for looking out for your bunk-mate when there's a bit of bother, eh?

It was everybody for themselves. Stuffing their desperate little souls into a lifeboat while Refdene is yelling to take it calm, get in and wait for the official boatmaster crew members to join them.

'The boatmasters will each take command of a lifeboat,' he's shouting over the clamour. 'Seal the hatch, and you will await their further instructions. All being well, it will be for a short while, until measures are taken—'

Measures were already being taken – the three boatmaster uniforms had forced themselves into the first shiny cylindrical boat, and the hatch was slotting itself snugly into place.

Mate Refdene was ranting at them – how vain do efforts come? The hatch was tight-locked. Next lifeboat was getting cramped up, too. And the third was opening up.

'In there,' he was pointing to us at the back, and the third boat. So we're scrambling in there just as the Klaxons picked up speed and volume to utterly an hysterical level, and there's red lights flashing on the hatches. 'They're closing,' he yells and dives into the second boat.

'What do we do now?' Ferty asks me as we're scrabbling into our wide choice of seats in Lifeboat Three. Ferty was on my canteen shift sometimes, so I knew him, sort of. And there was Dim Daine as well, from the next cubby room to me.

'Is this it?' We looked at each other. 'Just the three of us left?'

'And no boatmaster?'

'Shuggles!'

'The hatch's sealed itself, hasn't it? So what now?'

'We'll be auto-ejected if— Yoiks!' Huge, ship-trembling click, and a lurch, and a swaying motion to one side.

'We just been cast off,' Ferty said. '*Now's* the time to ask what happens next, because we haven't got a boatmaster. I bet none of us knows how to steer this thing.'

'I don't even know where we were heading.'

'I never even seen inside one of these things before.'

We looked at each other. 'Somewhere called Honorte. Big planet, low gravity, off the beaten spaceways for traders like us.' Ferty always knew things – Smarty-Farty, they call him sometimes.

 Eight days drifting.
At least we had plenty of space and stores.
As far as Ferty could tell, we were still heading for Honorte at the same speed as the Pride of Otton. Pride?

Huh – basic tramp trader and low-cost passenger shuttle, more like.

It was unfortunate, but expected, that none of us knew how to control the lifeboat.

'So we're in a bit of bother, then?'

Even so, we managed to make the rad-comm send and receive, and we thought we'd made an emergency bleep signal that appeared to be still operating.

'Haven't had any responses yet, though,' Daine was becoming morose.

'Not from the Fed, or the Pride of Otton, or any of the other lifeboats.' Ferty was heading for Despondency Pit.

'And we don't know anything about the Honortian life-forms?' I was getting a mite gloomy, too.

So we kinda sexed it up a bit. Er, all three of us. Well, as we all said, 'Who knows what the morrow will bring?'

Our morrow actually brought a touch of sorrow, because we were closing in on Honorte, and the autopilot informed us, 'Operation error. Main thrust engine identified as source of error. Closing down. Click.' And a long fading hum.

We looked at each other, 'I don't imagine anybody has read the manual on steering? Getting into orbit?'

'Can't be that hard, if a machine can do it,' ventured the less-than-bright Daine.

In theory, according to various red and white notices spread around the cabin and control section, it was a landable craft, which we thought meant it could perform a descent and come to a stable halt on the planetary surface.

'We could try to get into orbit, and wait for Fedhelp?'

'We should see if we manage any kind of orbit before we consider what happens after that.'

'We need to try something, or we'll go sailing past. The next planet could be ten trillion lyze away. The boat would be disintegral proton dust by then, never mind us.'

Our attempt to get into a stable orbit was, at best, pathetic and unsuccessful.

'It's not that bad,' Ferty congratulated me for having pressed every button in dozens of different sequences until that awful sleepy-sicky voice said, 'Orbit sequence initiated… click click click… Orbit sequence aborted. Thank you.'

So we took turns to scream at screens and kick at consoles, push buttons, twist little handlebar things and have sex. It seemed that something did respond to the handlebar apparatus and a set of pedals. 'It's like riding a cosmocar.' Ferty said, quite delighted in his seventh practise session.

'We'll wait for the Fed to turn up with rescue,' we agreed, having pooled our meagre, half-remembered knowledge about Honorte. Non-human. Past troubles had died down, but there was a general history of unrest-tending-to-violence between humans and the dominants there – the seaquans. 'Trade must be happening, or we wouldn't have been heading there.'

'I don't suppose any of us knows what our cargo for them was?'

No, we didn't. But we'd left it somewhere back in the void, anyway.

'It could be following us, spread around a thousand storage containers?'

'Best hope it's not dung, then.'

 The elliptical orbit we managed to establish wasn't as permanent as we'd hoped, even with the auto intermittently clicking in with, 'Orbit correction initiated. Orbit correction aborted.'
So Ferty took over... with me and Daine shouting encouraging advice, and having sex, until Ferty declared his satisfaction.

Or, actually, he stood up and said, 'The whole shugging thing keeps seizing up. Not responding at all. We'll have to leave it at that.' He brushed his hands together; we all high-fived – or high-foured in Ferty's right-hand case – and had sex to celebrate.

 We could see on three of the screens that the orbit wasn't stable. It was decaying, as they call it. The axes of the red ellipses around the sphere in the middle were becoming longer, and narrower. 'Which means,' Ferty explained to Daine, 'We're descending towards the upper atmosphere. Then we start to glow, and get banged about – and it's not sex. It's us on our terminal descent; and we'll be blown to bits and burned up after around seven minins.'

I talked Ferty into trying to steer us down, using the handlebars and pedals, which he swore were very slurkish and quite likely not responding at all by then, 'Except in my imagination.' But we strapped down and encouraged Ferty and cheered him on and watched the masses of sparks burying the visi screens, and masses of digits drowning data screens.

'I hope the natives are welcoming,' Daine croaked.

'As long as we get down in one piece to find out,' Ferty stuttered, gasped, and wrestled. No – that wasn't more sex, either – he was on the steering handlebar thing then.

'Shugger, shugger, shugger,' I said, feeling a new barrage of huge, rocking jolts, accompanied by a host of new sparks, squealing metal and shrieking Daine. *I just hope the natives aren't as dreadful as Ferty was saying. Maybe he's just been trying to scare me.*

 The crash must have been very spectacular from the outside. The noise was truly streme; plus all the slamming about, stomach-turning spins and horrible halt-slamming jerks. Better'n sex, I thought for a moment.

I was smashed and battered, and still strapped down in my chair. And the chair was still bolted to a section of plating. Half of Daine was on one side of me. I thought the red and gungy mess all over the control fascia must be Ferty.

Everything smelled of burning and blood and excrement. I thought a lot of that was me. But I couldn't move and undo the strapping and it was getting darker and I kept going all dark inside and couldn't think and see; and I could just feel, and I felt awful and so pained and wanting to cry and make it all go away.

 Something was there in the wreckage. I could hear it slithering. And slurping closer. And touching me. And interfering with me... like slinky slimy bits coming all over me and feeling me and in my clothes and horrible horrible – poking and prying and massaging like Foreplay Forster before they threw him in the brig. And I was hurting and crying and wanting it all to go away and stop and I could move my hands and arms a little bit and smack and push at it.

But it carried on poking me and sliding its slimy feelers all inside my clothes and probing me. *This isn't somebody come to rescue me.* Not rescue – it's robbery and fondling me; tentacles creeping and mauling all over me; making a howling sound. It keeps going tighter and pressing like Daine did sometimes, and I can't see it in the dark. It's something alien; and it's going to kill me, when it's mauled me to death first, pervy creature.

I struggled and thrashed and I knocked it over and it was still making that awful noise, and tentacles reaching all inside my clothes and I was half out the seat and struggling to get up and stop it and I found a soggy part that maybe felt like a head and I shook it and felt the tentacles gripping me more. I was screaming and shrieking at it and shaking it to stop it and telling it to leave me. I kept hitting the head part on something hard. I wanted to get away from it and couldn't move any more – still half-strapped down. Shuggery I felt terrible and pained and hurting everywhere and my eyes were stinging and I was fading black away again.

Some others were there and they had lights and I only got stark black and bright glimpses of them and they were touching me and one was talking and I could understand it… Asking why I'd done it.

'People are aghast,' it was saying. and I was wondering what about, like we had a choice about dropping out of orbit? Or in this place? Is it a special place? We smashed some special building down?

Others had come to see the wreck. I understood they were aghast as well.

'We're aghast,' they said when they heard what had happened.

 It seems… apparently… I've killed the local vet-doc. It – he – was attempting to repair me using their Kay-leetee philosophy, which involves the howling sounds, and terabytes of feeling and fingering, or whatever tentacles do. Tentling, I imagine, from the look of them.

So I'm in a bit of bother: I'm a murderer, and have been tried and found guilty. So swiftly done.

Public opinion, I'm told, is very much in favour of the ultimate penalty.

They're coming to explain "ultimate penalty" to me soon.

MY WIFE HAS THE FATTEST BACKSIDE

'My wife has the fattest backside you've ever seen.'

I was looking round. We'd arranged to meet here at Nine-o-nine. I hadn't seen him, but my ears pricked up now. I definitely know those tones.

'It is the biggest, most rounded, most distended—'

It got lost as I picked my way round the crush. But, yes, sounded like my hubby's voice amid the chinking of glasses.

'And her voice,' the unseen voice was saying, 'The shriekiest... Split your eardrums. On a par with a...' I think it compared me with Screaming Scarletta off the televids!

'Gordal Myti!' I heard that voice again – definitely my Charli. 'Spots? *Spots!* You never seen spots like'em this side of galactic centre.'

'As for her boo—' I lost a bit there in the babble: it's a noisy place on Virhday evenings, the public bar in the Laughing Limpet.

Then there was something about 'huge and red and ripe.' I don't know if he meant the spots or my backside.

Just wait till he gets over here with the drinks...

Patiently, I waited, forcing a smile to two other couples nearby. 'He's just so full of compliments these days, my Charli. Ahh, here he comes.'

I flubbered up, slapped my tail loudly, and waved a couple of flippers so he could see where I'd found a place. Just you wait...

I smiled more at the other two couples as Charli approached, bearing drinks and nibbles; and he hasn't forgotten his own smokes, of course.

'Oooh, Luv. You say the most wonderful things. Is my backside really that attractive? And my spots? Really turn you on, do they?' I glowed them up a bit, especially for the benefit of our drinking neighbours, all across my thorassia in radiating patterns, and settled down for a lovely romantic evening with my Charli.

WHO STARTED THE WAR?

'You what? You want to know who started the Humanics v Zouram war? The person, or zoug who actually started it?'

I gave her the look like she's out her nosy cerebrum if she thinks I know. Or if I'd tell her if I did. 'Obvious, isn't it?' I said. 'The guy who pushed the Fire button on the Krord of Leation's weapon-pods.'

'Actually, it was a female who—'

'Typical woman, huh? Always starting the bother.' Thought I might as well diss her off; no skin off my toes. 'You getting the drinks in, if you want to talk to me?' I gazed at my drink four-pot, less than half full.

'I wasn't intending—'

'Nor was I. I come in the Deep Dive Bar and Smokery to drink, inject, absorb, space out, breathe it in – anything from anal philosophy on Mejur to eighty-percent calahol from Polik. It's quite something in here – worth coming a long way for – there's an atmosphere like Voltana some nights.'

She was giving me that what-the-duck look by then.

'You heard of somebody getting the DDBs, haven't you?' I carried on. 'This is what it means – spending a day in here, the DDB Smokery.'

Lady-with-the-nose was looking down it, so I iced her and waved to Jerri, mi mate with the open cred card at the bar. He was trying to be noticed in the company of a pair of Angle-heads in his gold-sheen pseudo-jacket – Spacie-wannabe. So he kinda waved, a bit ostentatious, and was happy to cred me a drink if it made him look like one of the in-crowd. I watched one section of my four-pot fill up nicely, and touched my commipad – *Jez – chat with you later.*

But Nosey Lady was all contrition then; trying to make up for it – a quick drink tapped into the other empty section; a glad-eye in Jerri's direction; and a stroke down my thigh. 'Tell me about Chatty; you knew Chatty, didn't you? Knew him well, I've heard?' She had this devious I-know-everything look about her. Silly woman. All pegged-up like a parrot on a perch in this feather-plaz suit. I tell you, fashion on Periquito has a lot to answer for these days. It's not as if you don't hallucinate in a place like DDBs, anyway, without people dressing up like your nightmares.

'Chatty?' I said. 'What about him?'

Krordy-Dee – she thinks she knows it all. So, why not? Might as well bill the squeens on the matter. After all – a), it's largely of academic interest now, and b), she's got the wrong end of the dick. Plus c), she's still stroking my leg, and, oh, yes – d), she's just ordered more Chateau Kännissä for me.

'Right,' I said. 'Well, Chatty was ideally placed at the time—'

'No. Before that. I want to know *all* about him. From a long time back. What led up to the war.'

I thought about it… Could I spin out the drinks-buying for a worthwhile period? 'Okoi. You want a bit of background? From *The Beginning?*'

She gave me that look that said she didn't believe I was at *The Beginning*, like the me-and-God, hand-in-hand beginning, "Let there be $E=mc^2$" sort of *Beginning.*

'Very well,' I decided, 'everything I recall from back then?'

She pushed the smoke-pack my way. That was level-devil: for a pack of Keiju Savu, I'd think of something to tell her about. Clamping my fingers over the pack, I had no intention of letting them go once I started.

'Chatty,' I started, 'was always talkative, almost right from birth on Al'Fritton. He couldn't help himself. Didn't really try, I suppose. Once he began speaking, there was no stopping him.'

'But he wasn't called Chatty then?'

'Yes, he was. Maybe not his born-with, real name, but he re-registered himself Chatty. I mean who would willingly be called Laiha Rotta? It means something like Skinny Rat in the Ulvroon language. Especially for a man. *Laiha?*'

Nosey Lady gave me the blanks.

'It means *fairy* in Lutese,' I explained. 'Like, you know – *Laiha nuuska?*' And I did the pervy wiggle to make it even more plain.

That was wasted on her. She was sitting there like Gorda Mydi and didn't even get a triple-meaning, tri-lingual joke in Lute, Ulvroon and Stang. Ah, well, the drinks and smokes were on tap and flue, so I was happy enough to chatter with her about almost everything I recalled of those days. *Could spin this into a long night,* I was thinking, *if she keeps up with this rate of supply. Cheap night. Must come here again.*

'Chatty's family re-homed to Bolso,' I started up again. 'That's a much more peaceable planet, in terms of geology, earthquakes and volcanic ways. At the education centre near his new home, he was the star talker – in the class booths, to teachers, in the play areas – to everyone.

'Oh, yes; Chatty was always the one for a cheery greeting, lingering discussion, or an interruption; never an argument. He simply didn't listen to anyone else; he just talked, and was always happy. Didn't matter whether or not anyone was listening. Chatting was his *razon debtor*.

'He inadvertently talked his way into many a bed. The girls just loved his chatter about anything and everything. Not that he chatted them up with that specific intention, they just liked him. Probably took him to bed to shut him up, but it never worked. Er, from what I heard… saw… that is. Nothing would shut him up for long.'

My plastic-plumage-clad lady finger-touched at a 'corder now and again. A bit distracting, that. But to be expected. Presumably, she was doing the asking and paying for a reason. Someone would be paying and expensing her. So much the better, really. *You just carry on tip-tapping the smokes and hoosh, my feathery provider, and we'll get on alright.*

'It was the same at the higher ed centres.' I finished my third Savu and Kännissä. 'Chatty learned techno engineering the real way – by long-exposure study – gained plenty of experience out in the wild; and drained every memo they had. Plus talking with everyone who'd listen and answer, which was pretty much a full-time occupation – there were plenty of other students around, from all over the sector – dozen different planets and languages.

'Regardless of shape or shade, species or speech badge, he could never resist greeting anyone he met, or passed by, or happened to meet on the screens and links; streets and blinks. So he had to learn a star-map-full of quick-chat lines, didn't he? In case they answered, and asked him something in Azerjab or Zulist. Between times, he picked up a couple or more languages on the drip-head memos.'

'Picked them up? You don't just "pick up" three languages.'

'Yes, okoi; three all-night memo-sessions with each. He took to them, didn't get the usual headaches. Also absorbed more high-tech ones.'

'Clever fella, Chatty. Military, as well, hmm?' That hand my thigh was stroking just nicely; and my drink had just self-topped-up again. So all was well.

'He was pretty much absorbed with the techno-combative aspects, so when he was offered a chance to study military technology first hand – in the real, instead of total-memo – and even help to create new memo-drops, he leapt at it. Even gave a twenty-minute acceptance speech that was expected to be simply a "Thank you". But this is Chatty we're talking.

'Then when the military assignment was completed, he took up a post with the space force techno development staff out on Stokko, where they got that mini-black hole under observation. Course, he talked them all to death between shifts.'

I had to smile at some of the memories from back then. 'Eh, that place... Chatty fitted in like a jig in a saw.'

Nosey Feathers checked the 'corder was getting all this; made a pen-tab note, and nodded to the hoosh, as if I needed reminding that heaven lay before me in a four-pot drinkery.

'Then he had the chance of a promotion transfer, and a move to Crich, that fringe planet on the Oston inner rim. It was his near-driven-to-deafness fellow staff who clandestinely volunteered him for the post, so he was a little surprised at the seeming offer from the black. But he accepted it willingly, looking forward to double-money, and a new group of friends to greet and chat with, discuss so many new topics with. A whole new gamut of colleagues and chat companions.'

'He didn't suspect they were just getting rid of him?'

'Apparently not. But the reality wasn't quite what he expected, once he'd rattled and chattered his way through the first forty days of introduction to the work in the crowded Crich Base Station 2.

'Commodore Skuff called him into the SuprOps Room. "That's your trial period concluded, Chatty. We've considered your qualifications and aptitudes, and all the training you've had; your expertise, skills, ability with absorbing techno-head drops and memos. And we've decided on your ideal placement for the next two years. You know two languages, do you?"'

'"Five fluent. Passable in eleven," he told him.

'Commodore said they only needed him fluent in Matlok and Chessy at the Stokko Centre, but they'd found a perfect placement for his skills in military technology as well as languages, so his next assignment would be Oddrich.'

'Oddrich? Where's that?' Feathers pulled a beak... er, face, and paused in her fingering of the 'corder.

'That's what Chatty said. But Commodore Skuff said, "Never mind where it is. Rather secret, the exact locality; military, you know. Our supericon shuttle will drop you off. Your departure will be in two days. Eight of you are going to your new postings, one person per post. Good luck."

'When he got there, dropped off on a one-man shutter, he found he was alone. It was a deep-space station orbiting nowhere. The nearest star was little more than a dot. No planets, comets or rogue objects. The whole vast nothingness was there, and he was in it, alone, and silent.

'"What am I doing here?" he asked, when he got a link, seven days later.

'"Listening. All eight of you are on fringe patrol. You're just listening for aliens – no, we've never heard any yet, but you never know. Just monitor the vac-waves. Anything that comes in, relay it back to us. Never attempt to reply. There's no auto-acknowledgement – we don't want any aliens out there to know we exist, do we? Much less to locate our whereabouts. Don't worry, it'll never happen – hasn't in the twenty-seven years we've had these listening stations.'

'*"Twenty-seven years?"* Chatty was utterly aghast. "Twenty-seven years without anyone or anything to talk to?"

'"We're cautious. You never know. Don't worry about it. Do the checking on the auto systems. A year'll go in no time."

'*"A year?"* he said, totally smab-gocked at the appalling prospect of no-one to chat with for a whole Schmooking year! And very limited Post to Base contact – so no secret buddy to chew the chuxy with.'

'So how did he manage to start the war out there? Crich fringe posts are utter-outer.' She sneaked a quick sip of something out of her bag, but sniffed when I asked about sharing whatever it was. 'Anti-hoosh,' she said. 'It keeps me moderately sober – I'm working.'

I mean, that proves she was ratted – admitting it like that.

'There you go,' I said, 'assuming, same as everybody else. Anybody ever prove Chatty started the war? So don't give me all that supposition bit. All this presumption of guilt is making me double-thirsty, so you want to give Bixy a wave, huh?'

We waited for moderate, musing moments while the music started up with some Wekmudd Melodies – you know the sort of stuff – all twanging strings and 4T cadences – okay if you're in the mood. Not tonight, well-spaced, thinking back to them days.

'So,' I said. 'He had no Base contact. They made sure of that; they didn't want their outlier monitors spending all day every day chatting back instead of concentrating on the back-vac, did they? So there was no routine link to Base. Just an emergency connection that he had to code into if he picked up anything of interest from Further Out. And that, of course, had to be switched on before it worked. If it was live all the time, it would have been getting in touch every five minins with feedback from the in-hub music and voice system. So for him, it was total silence, talk-wise. Background music? Huh; big choice. So he was talking to the musician holographs like they were really there.'

'Philosophising with a Calician trombosolist wouldn't be exactly stimulating, I suppose,' Nosey Feathers was sympathetic on that.

'Might be if the next best thing was a female singaster from Kerrith. But, anyway, it didn't last long. Twenty-one days, and Chatty picked up an unknown signal that really was from somewhere Further Out. But it was nothing to relay back – could have been a PS echo; or lensing signal; maybe random flutter-noise. So he did a lot of monitoring and tuning in; picked it up more.

'He decided it was a voice. Worked on it, got it clear. Sounded a bit like Darbee speech—'

'So, being Chatty, he just had to answer back?'

'Ah – you got me there. Exactly. I mean, he was totally the wrong guy to put out there. He was never going to keep quiet and listen to them, and then pass it all on to somebody else to deal with. It would be someone with no idea of the true purity of nattering who would start communication with them, talking, signalling back, whatever they were doing.

'These signals coming in could have been just domestic, trader, military chatter for all he knew. Absolutely no reason at all why it would be aimed at him. He was merely listening-in, monitoring, making sure it was truly new stuff, not some echoing reflections or lens-effect, something like that.

'It was inevitable, with no-one to talk to, that Chatty talked more and more to himself, figuring it all out in his head, trying to make sense of it, listening to the incoming chatter and mentally analysing it. He began to pick up some meanings in it; like, soaking in—'

'Absorbing it?'

'Yeah; a few words seemed to be common with some Ulvroon dialect. He puzzled and practised, answering in his head, repeating, wandering round the hub of his station endlessly, muttering and pretending, exaggerating his alien accent and possible phrases in their speech, embellishing, putting on the style with flamboyant gestures, making up for his lost twenty days of near silence.

'He didn't see much point reporting to Base, so, maybe sulking, he didn't bother.' I checked up in her direction, see if she was still following this.

'He must have left a circuit open one day, and didn't realise that his echoing was being re-broadcast, back to the source of the chatter. Wherever it was.

'Then he received a direct reply a day later. It corrected his pronunciation of *awwhkadbkddh asa jaksis, Shatty-Ssjhh?* which seemed to translate in his mind as "What the fuck you saying, Chatty-Alien?"

'From this, he deduced that they understood at least some of what he was saying – enough to have garnered his name from his ramblings; and they were a sexual species, or they wouldn't cuss like that; and they had a sense of humour, or they wouldn't have said that. Additionally, they weren't desperate to progress up the hierarchy, or they would have said, "Take me to your Leader."

'So, clearly, they were content with Chatty – maybe they didn't know about ranks and the importance of self-importance in the military.'

'Don't let the Gold Braid hear you think that.' She had this dire smile and ignored my hand on her knee. So that was alright.

'Me? I'm out of it. They got no jurisdiction on me.'

'They don't need it; they can extend as far as they like, to anyone. You know that.' And stubbed her smoke out on the back of my hand as I tried to slide a fraction higher. I withdrew my good feelings about her, until the next drink, anyway.

'Yeah, well, anyway. So Chatty's live conversations began, and he was in his element – dialoguing...

conversing... discussing... dissertating and jus' plain nattering.'

'And Base never noticed?'

Well, you shrug to a daft question like that, don't you? 'Of course they didn't notice. Too glad to be rid of him and his eternal chatter, I imagine. They weren't going to keep a line open for him, were they? Out of sight; out of earshot. If he had anything to report— Well, I mean, there had been nothing for twenty-seven years, had there? So they weren't holding their dix, were they?'

Feathers didn't have any answer to that.

'So, he was getting on great with them – up day and night – such as it is on a drift-post to nowhere. Talking, sharing, informing and gleaning. And some zoug out there was as talkative as he was—'

'Did he call them that? Zougs?'

'Just seemed right – it was a common sound in their diction-repertoire – and they sure knew how to communicate in it.'

'So he couldn't get a phrase in sideways?'

'Far from it. Seemed like natural turn-taking, him and this usual zoug-guy. Perfect for each other; ideal conversationalists. Intermeshed, not clashed.'

'That's not what Fed Military said about it.'

I mean – you just got to lose all faith in anyone who gives what Fed said any cred, don't you? But I din't say anything to her – just gave her the Dozy-You look.

'So they were chatting on about this and there, here and where, a bit beyond and further yet—'

'Until Fed Base realised?'

'Mmm. Took them more than a hundred days. An auto-monitoring link patched itself in for an upgrade, download, listen-in, plus health and sanity check. They heard him chatting, and answering himself. Two days later, they realised it wasn't him in a two-way self-conversation: there was someone else in there with him.

'Three further days, and they realised the truth: he was chatting with some unknown species way out in the Big Black Yonder.'

She was perking up a bit. I thought I was boring her up to then. But this was the main focus-point she wanted the up-down on. So I took my time over a sniff and sip.

'Well? What did he do? Insult them? Declare a private war? Start a species-trafficking club? Crucify their plenipotentiaries?'

'Do you have to believe all the Fed-Crap? They would say that, wouldn't they?'

'They would, yes. And they did. And lots of other things about him. It's the time he disappeared. It all fits – Fed executed him for "Traitorous activities causing compromise to our boundary regions, and culminating in the breakout of war with the Zouram".'

'Fid they Duck. Fed couldn't get near him. No scheduled trip that way for two-hundred-plus days, at the earliest. No spare pop-out-and-see craft. So Chatty was just yelled at.

"For ducksake, you idiot – you'll have given your position away..."

"You could have been attacked..."

"They could have traced Fed Base..."

"You're demoted."

"You'll be lucky if you ever rise above Genital Private."

General Pilikia and a host of subordinates ranted at him in some no-back-chat rollicking session over the vac-waves.'

'What' She was not believing this. 'They let him carry on?'

'Oh, no. They didn't exactly permit him: they couldn't stop him. Couldn't physically get at him, but he was very strongly ordered to never speak again, to remove the link, to listen only, and make some effort to locate the source of the chatter.'

'Er... if he removed the link, he wouldn't be able to listen in? Or trace it.'

'Exactly. And Chatty being Chatty, he couldn't obey impossible orders – like Never speak again. Recognising the stupidity of everything they said, and the futility of attempting to obey any of it, he cut the link to Fed Base instead, and apologised to his ethereal friends for his eight-day silence, and warned it might happen again if Fed Base re-became stroppy with him.

'Next thing he knows, middle of a late-shift conflab, they told him there wouldn't be any more problems with his Base. No more interference from them.'

'What?' Feathery Nose pops up. 'That was when Fed Base Six was eliminated? Because the aliens didn't like Chatty being shouted at and upset?'

'Yes, that was about it. Of course, it couldn't continue. Fed would have retaliated, but they didn't know where to attack. They eventually managed to spare three ships and come out to Oddrich post. They took over; and issued the most unimaginable doom-warning threats in the most broken Zouram you could imagine; and two of the ships started off towards the even-further-out rim sector, looking for them.'

'So… they'll be the two ships that were vapped?' Her little fingers were a blur on the mini kb.

'Guess so.'

'And the war started?'

'Wasn't much of a war, was it? Fed had no idea who they were fighting, or where they were. They just had m— *Chatty* as a prisoner. And some unknown alien power… civilisation… running vectors round them, demanding Chatty's re-instatement as the liaison contact with the Fed.'

'If they could do all that, their technology must be centuries ahead of ours. The things they must have command of – awesome – the power at their fingertips—'

'Er, *tentacle*-tips, I think you'll find. And yes, their power and capabilities are immensely impressive. I used to imagine them, out in the streets, or battering their pressure-pads with their nostrilly-paws, demanding, "We want Chatty". Or maybe scrawling it on the curves of the next sonic sub-ducer they propelled in the Fed's direction.

'So? Chatty? What happened to him? They got rid of him? Found a replacement?'

'Bit of everything, I suppose, but it took time. Fed lost two more vessels on what they called "aggressive intersection trajectories" with wherever they thought the Zourams might be.'

'Ah, but we destroyed eleven of their craft, and several bases – even a moon-base—'

'Fiddle-dee-duck! Fed had no idea where they were, or what their vulnerabilities were.'

My feathery-plumed lady friend caught on real slow, 'You mean… they made it all up? About the hostilities?'

'Weren't really hostilities. More like chastisement of a wilful child. In the nature of a little smack to make it behave. A midweight destroyer, or was it a Cee-Class Light Attack vessel? One of ours, anyway, vanished in a cloud of protonic plasma.'

'No, no,' she protested. 'That wasn't the extent of the war. The Zouram lost several vessels. We raided their bases—'

'Rubbish. All invented for the newscasts – tried to make it sound like a mutual victory and convenience. Fed lost one major base and four ships they don't talk about. And blame Chatty for starting it with all his flabber-mouthing?'

'But... but you're saying... all along, it was our gold braid trying to shut him up that sparked it off?'

'Precisely.' Credit where it's due – in Chatty's lap.'

'Not exactly a War, then, was it?'

'Indeed not. They merely removed some Fed craft that had come seeking, and repeated their request to resume relations with Chatty.'

'So?'

'It was that; or they ceased communications altogether. Or there'd be a real, full-zapping war, which they showed they were pretty good at already.'

'So Fed didn't want to lose touch with a powerful alien empire; or federation? And knew they couldn't win a serious war against them?'

'Right.' Ah, she was getting it pretty clear now, and I was getting a refill in my four-pot. Great place this.

'Chatty? He wasn't executed, like they always said?'

'Face-saving propaganda by Fed Central. The Zouram were so glad to hear him again, in one coherent piece, and meet him the flesh, they didn't want to risk losing him again—'

'What? Just because he chatted with them a lot?'

'There's no "just" about it. Chatting is an art form with them. They regarded him as a connoisseur. Plus, he was an alien one. And a key to eleven other Federation languages—'

'Which they could use in ill ways?'

'Course they could. But they were pretty adamant about it being him, and going to Zouram, the planet, in person. Only they call it Exx'ommo'oddon. Fed saw the situation, and they insisted as well, so I had to go, eventually—'

'*You* had to? You mean? *You?*'

I had to smile. '*E hele mai, señota. Cum aş şti totul dacă? Wa sore o nasıl bilebilirim? Alfa Kimse?* Which, as you'll no doubt know, roughly translated from Regone, means, "Come on, Lady, how the uffle would I know all that if I was Alfi Nobody?"'

'*You? You're Chatty?*'

I had to smile a little more as I helped myself to the needle that had just appeared. 'No need to sound so incredulous. You *must* have suspected?'

She was still looking like she'd never believed it – thicker than I'd thought.

'Fed and the Zouram jointly appointed me Ambassador Primary and Extraordinary – Ape, for short – for six years. Everybody had to listen to what I said. Life on Exx'ommo'oddon is great. I learned to drink like a local. And Boy – can those guys slurp it back.'

'There's still an Ape, er, ambassador out there. So who is it now?'

'Have you not coddled-on yet? With Zouram technology being so vastly in advance of ours – or *yours*, as I tend to think of it these days? It's still me out there. You don't think you're talking with a real person here, do you? I'm a solido-sensory hologram. I regularly visit here for recreation and research. Zouram tech really is rather wonderful, you know.

'The real Chatty me is a zillion yonks away.' I looked round at my tentacled mates on Exx'ommo'oddon, with their kutush frills all over the place, 'in a bar very much like this one.

'But I like this place a lot, too.' I helped myself to another large swigfull of her drinks, 'Besides, drinking here is so much cheaper than back home.'

ME, PROF AND A TAIL TO TELL

'It's all going beautifully, Prof,' I told him as we looked into the trench where we'd been digging the night before. 'The weather's holding. So are the sun shades, and so's our health.'

I'm only Second-in-Department, but I'm enthusiastic, full of suggestions, and eagerly helpful. The more I'm like that, the better for both of us.

'I won't last forever,' Prof told me last year. 'So keep it up, and come with me on next summer's dig in Africa. It'll be a geology-cum-early-humans dig I've always wanted to do. Support me on this, and the post's yours when I retire. Won't be long, Adrian. Promise.'

Fine by me; I'm keen anyway, so none of this was any hardship. All going well out there on the dig, especially having confirmed it was the right kind of level and strata for early humans.

'Pre-human remains haven't previously been found in this region,' Prof sold me on the expedition, 'but the age of these rocks is the same as those at Olduvai Gorge, in Tanzania.

'Officially, this is Late Miocene in age, but I think of it, rather hopefully, as Anthropocene – the Early Man Level.'

'So we're hopeful speculators?'

Now, looking into the trench, we were still undecided on the balance between hopeful and successful. The single tooth and bone fragment we found two weeks back was the highlight so far. Meagre, but possibly significant, as initial analysis didn't match it with anything known.

'Might be a new sub-species of human,' we wondered, but not too positively.

The students left yesterday, partly because the heavy digging work was largely over, and partly because they were going to a festival in Stockhill for the week before term restart.

So this was our first day without them, on our own, and we went down to check on a half-centimetre piece of bone-like rock – it's a distinct dark ivory colour with associated smooth surface texture. It was protruding – if you can call half a centimetre of anything protruding – from the western edge of the shallow trench we'd dug across that section of the valley floor. Even that was proving to be hard work in this heat, especially with the tough and tangled roots that infested the ground.

We both know the technique so well: trowel off the over-burden fairly cautiously, and sieve everything. Then get even more careful as we work our way lower, towards the target. Then dental picks and brushes as we get close on top of the target. By which time our excitement level is generally through the canopy roof,

'It's either going to be an ape fingertip, or something like a horse or dog-bear – like hemicyon.'

I was right. Spot on. Not an ape, and not an equus or hemicyon, either. Or a ground sloth or mastodon. But it was, most definitely, a fingertip. Right behind it was the rest of the finger.

By noon-time siesta, we had the hand! Me and Prof were both gasping in awe, 'The biggest, best preserved and most complete, articulated set of any pre-Pleistocene anthropoid bones found anywhere in the world, *ever.*'

We looked at each other in total amazement and awe and everything else that means gob-smacked. 'The enormity of it, Young Adrian.'

That was the longest, best, hottest and everything-else day of my life to date – well, maybe equal with the day The Honourable Sophie Wallingham-Smythe insisted that she was my room-mate for the term.

Prof doesn't drink, but he did that night. 'And there's no sign of it ending there, Young Adrian,' he kept saying. He's not used to Tusker beer and Cape Town Whisky chasers, although, at the time, he was referring to the bones, not the drink.

Speculation was the spectre over the banquet that night. Might there be a part of an arm? How would it end? A break? Chewed off by predators? Scavengers? Complete with teeth marks? Or disarticulated at the wrist or elbow?

It was like wildest-imagination's ultra-dream that there could be part of the actual body there.

But there it was – the shoulder bone! Then, an hour of stupefied scraping, and – the scapula. And the clavicle. 'That's the whole shoulder,' Prof's hugging me like a nutter.

'Ribs!!! It's never going to end.' We suppressed the desperate urge to lie on the ground and kiss every inch of it.

'We'd have dusty lips, and no mistake.'

'All the more reason for another beer.' Prof was getting the idea of drink.

'It's not even crushed completely flat; there's a semi-roundedness about it. Like one-and-a-half D instead of 3D.'

So far, there wasn't a single bone missing, and we had the whole upper body. The skull, left arm and right leg were exposed.

'It doesn't match any of the known subspecies of early humans. Thirteen parameters – differences on all of them, beyond what can be explained by individual-person variations; gender differences; or mere chance.'

'This line of teeth looks like they could be a necklace.'

'So, our find was wearing a trophy of some carnivore of the times?' we mused. 'Most likely a bear, judging by the size and shape of these teeth.'

Prof had the scribblings for his paper well drafted out. We agreed that he would do most of the writing, and I would do the visual recordings – stills, videos and drawings. And we'd share the credits and the mapping.

Then came the bombshell. I'd half-expected to find the Big Joke, like a plastic card engraved with the names of all the festival-going group, but this. 'This confirms it's a hoax,' we agreed.

'He's got a bloody tail.'

That night was a kind of desperate-cum-muted affair, arguing over the possible fakery of this one and all the others around the world and the ages. Against the absolute authenticity of the bones we had – the structure, the bone material, condition, the humanoid features of the skull – no exact match to any known group, but positively within the realms of very early human.

'Not all that "very early",' we agreed when we went through the data and measurements and replays. 'These really are the remains of an extremely feasible early human. Complete.'

'Sure – complete with a three-metre tail.'

'Bit of a bummer, that.' We drank to doubt and indecision.

Next morning, we pulled the tarp off the site – all five-by-five metres of it, including the coiled tail. 'It impresses the shit out of me,' said Prof. 'I can't see where the joins are, as they say. That tail is a direct and seamless continuation of the spine – curling outwards, instead of hooking under, like the coccyx.'

'The whole skeleton is faultless. Too perfect to be a fake. Look at the junction of the whole spinal base area – it's absolutely textbook. Every bone fits exactly. All the ilium… pubis… ischium structures are… well, perfect.'

'If,' I said, 'this is not a fake. That means it is real. Genuine. Which is totally unexpected, impossible and unprecedented. That is what we need to decide, write up, publicise, and challenge all-comers to tell us where we went wrong in the normal peer-review process.'

It took Prof some time to ponder it over, but the eventual decision, was, 'You're right, Adrian. We'll let the world decide, and if we're wrong, they can laugh and tell us where our error is.'

Our term didn't start on time. We remained out there for two months while we organised the finances for a crew to come and help us protect it, lift it, and get it onto the transporter. Evenings, Prof and I worked on the presentations for the journals, the internet, our sponsors in the museum and university, and several releases for newspapers and television programmes.

The Uni, the museum and the Tanzanian government were reserving decisions on who would take charge of the final preparation and eventual display of the actual specimen, depending on its verification as world-astoundingly genuine.

The flight back to the UK was a huge period of anticipation and semi-suppressed excitement. We were jointly interviewed by half-a-dozen agencies, a mix of sceptical, sarcastic and jesting, but all waving their copies of our press release.

Then Prof went off with the Uni lot, probably to negotiate his salary and expenses, in light of a) being two months late for his lecturing duties; and b) being the possibly biggest star or embarrassment the place had ever known.

And I went home to The Honourable Sophie Davison-Wallingham-Smythe.

It was the next day, or the one after, that I rang Prof to see how he was faring with the drizzly cold UK after all the drought and heat out there. But his wife said he'd gone for a walk the previous evening, and not come back. And there'd been a robbery at their home that morning – all his papers and computers taken.

'He said he was going to ring you, to confirm the arrangements for the arrival and collection of the specimen.'

'Oh? It was supposed to be here two days ago.' That was puzzling.

'That's what he thought, but it seems not to have arrived at Heathrow.'

'Oh.' We chatted worriedly for a moment or two, and she rang off, each of us promising to contact the other in the event of any news.

Oh, indeed. Prof's vanished? And all our direct evidence in the form of the actual remains, the originals of the paperwork, computer files, diaries, site maps and logs?

'Doesn't sound good,' I told Sophie.

'Might he have spirited the fossil and himself away, to claim sole glory?' she wondered aloud.

'Can't imagine that, but…' Well, some profs have been known to double-cross their helpers and students for their last chance of personal glory. 'No, not Prof. He wouldn't,' and I wandered out.

Ding ding ding. The bell started playing Theme from Rocky.

'I'll get it. Someone at the door,' I called back to Sophie.

***

I'll be in here for at least another two months. It seems like that long already. Cervical fractures can be a long time in the recovery, especially when the throat and everything in it is crushed, as well as two vertebrae.

Talk about lucky. The ambulance guys who came for me had just undertaken their latest training on intubation for breathing in casualties such as mine.

'Sod-alone knows how you did it,' they said to me. 'Kept breathing unaided for that long… lungs half-full of blood.'

'Chuffing Nora knows how you did it,' the surgeon said to the ambulance two.

'Only the Good Lord Above knows how you did it,' the Honourable Sophie said to the surgeon. 'But my eternal thanks and prayers are with you.' She's like that, is Sophie. My little saint.

The couple who were at the door that day looked perfectly normal. I was just suspicious about their spiel on the doorstep – it reeked of internet scam. Vague knowledge, promises, semi-threats.

What convinced me that something was wrong was the tail – all ten feet of it – that whipped out and lashed itself round my neck, and tightened. I felt the cartilage crushing, my breathing choking off. Seeing the eyes and thinking there was nothing different about them. No glittering facets or even a red glow as the dark curtains came around.

It sounds like my office at the uni, and at home, got the same treatment as the Prof's – robbed bare and wrecked while Sophie and the kids were overseen by the woman visitor, as they wisely cowered in the playroom.

The big difference between me and the Prof – apart from his exalted rank and "missing" status – is that I do the internet, computers, cctv, cloud file storage, and endless backups of every document, photo or film I ever produced. Including, naturally, the security cameras covering my front door and the hallway; not to mention the YI kiddi-watch camera in the playroom.

So all the evidence, apart from the actual bones and bedrock, still exists in electronic form. I have cleared it all for release, and I understand that my home cctv coverage and kiddi-cam stuff is out today on the telly.

I wonder two things: firstly, How will they explain the tail that flashed from the man's clothing and tightened around my neck; and a very similar tail that cracked like a whip in the playroom?

The second little wondering I have is, Will they be more efficient if they have another go at me?

I'M NOT PERFECT YET

Okay, so I'm not perfect yet. I know I need help and guidance on some matters from time to time. But, with much effort, I am improving.

Taking four large breaths, I stood in the exact centre of the inner foyer, where Eldirk, my aide, said would be ideal. He remained by my side as I waited for my guest to arrive. I was self-conscious in the middle of all that mirror glass and satin chrome, with so little comforting red carpet, but I did it with Eldirk's helping hand squeezing mine twice.

'This is he,' Eldirk whispered. 'Smile now.'

My baby-faced visitor recognised me, small smile and wave. He hugged me in greeting, and I stood and let him. Arms by my side, and closed my eyes and pouted my lips in reciprocation. *There. That was all correct.* I had trained and practised until I had reached that standard and toleration level. I was moderately pleased that I had done it.

Eldirk leaned to me, 'You were great.'

Thereafter, we got on acceptably well, although Baby-face was a little brash and too hands-on-feely for me. Touched my leg a couple of times. *Too much. Too much.* Too big a smile – a bit false. Even I sensed that. But we conducted the business – my aide doing all the notes, recordings and supportive murmurs.

By the end of the day, the deal was pretty much fixed. It merely needed our signa-seals, in eight days, while the whole thing was made neat, and had the compulsory pause time.

Except. I heard Baby-face chuntering as he went out, talking with his companion in the su-lift about, 'What a scappy scudder she is. She didn't even return my greeting.

'See how she didn't shake hands with me on the way out?

'Huh, wouldn't have a drink…

'Never smiled.

'I'm having nothing to do with that bleak bitch again… well, only for the preferential rates she's giving us.

'Like a Friego fish, she is. Wait till I tell the others about her.'

I listened as he faded away, still whingeing to his silent escort.

It was disappointing – didn't he even glance at the pre-notes? About me being a Frozen. I can't do those things, not like I used to. Since the Vitros took me prisoner out on Pool – the 90% water planet in the DV sector. Four years ago, when I was running mixed cargoes and setting up small-scale engineering projects. The Vitros fancied experimenting on me, as part of their research on humans.

I ended up like this – can't move much. I'm still me, but my muscle control is via the drugs, electros and parafits – and they're not perfected yet – even with my moderate financial resources.

I am improving. My intelligence never wavered, nor my sanity – though it was Butch and Flo at times. My metabolism and neuro-reactivity are just on different wavelengths now. A mite slow with the physical responses. A bit mismatched. My emotions and spontaneity aren't fully returned yet.

I know I'm not perfect yet: it's all there in the brief pre-notes, so people know what to expect when they come visiting. It wasn't easy to get myself back this well. Nor to compile the notes – laying myself bare like that – *and he never bothered to snick through them.*

So, till the boffins have perfected me, I'll simply have to carry on being the sort of vindictive emotionless vengeful murdering *scavitch* the Vitros created. The kind of dispassionate iceberg who'll poison any ignorant *shuyuck* who treats her with a total lack of understanding. Like that *spregavole* turd who just went deprecatingly out the door.

Chào quixin, as the Vitros used to tell me: 'Say hello to the devil.' I can feel my blood coming to the boil. He's back in eight days for the signing. I'll have a little something ready for him…

a small celebratory meal…
    a drink to seal the deal…
        his funeral.

ROMANCE ON THE ROCKS

'There's one thing about Outer Space, Jess: it's big. And it's black. And it's empty.'

'That's three things, Zeke.' She stared at him, *You've got that eager little face on, haven't you? You're after something, that's for sure. What's your angle this time?*

There was always something with Zeke, which was why she'd only agreed to meet him in a public place, the Phobos Bar, in the Tharsis Terminal. It was the busiest orbital hub in the Solar System.

The view of the Acidalia Planitia, on the Martian surface, 36kk below, was spectacular for newcomers. *Over-enhanced as far as regulars are concerned,* she thought, *but pleasant enough while I waited for him.*

The bar was crowded. Her companion fitted well among the multi-coloured panels and polished chrome fittings, gyrating lights and almost no gravity. Zeke was equally common and brightly plaz; lit-up half the time; and you wouldn't trust him as far as you could launch him. Still wearing that slightly quizzical smile that tells you he's constantly checking to see if you believed the last thing he said.

'I warned you last time, Zeke,' she told him. 'I'll kill ya if you screw me about again. You got to be straight with me. I'm well past putting up with you messing me ever again.'

'Mmm, yes. Course.' He reached to hold her hand. 'Er, I meant four. I forgot to mention the other thing about space: I own a little bit of it. It's an asteroid. I'm the "Legal and Rightful Registered Owner in Law." It says so on my certificate, which can be viewed on the space-web under *Myspace/asteroid-belt/quad08-278914. EarthGov.sw'*

'Yeah, yeah, I know the legals, Zeke. What about it?' Jessamyne knew him well enough to realise that her on-off lover would have an obtuse angle somewhere – he was never solicitous unless he was deep in plotting something devious.

'It's a 1.8k max-diam lump of rock floating around the outer periphery of the Hildian Group, one of the dynamicals in a 3.2 resonance group with Jupiter – you know how they class and group the asteroids, officially, yes?'

She nodded wearily, 'Depending which memo you last soaked in – yours is classed among the *stable-dynamical* class, is it?'

Pleased she was at least listening, he offered her a drink at the 'spenser. 'With sub-classes about accessibility, position and size. Complicated business—'

'Zeke! Hush the technicals – we've both been surveying stroids for more'n a decade. What are you after? I came specially to see you, so don't be wasting my time.' *Not entirely true: I'm resting up between assignments and had nothing better to do than chew the oxy with a very long-term so-called friend. But trust him? No chance.*

'I bought it on a hunch-cum-calculation about ten years ago,' Zeke took his time – she was here now, and wouldn't float off on an impatient whim. 'I worked out that it properly belonged in the collision class, not the dynamicals. By *my* calculations it stood an 87% chance of colliding with another of the un-catalogued bodies, which were counted as anything less than 2k across back then.'

'Get to it, Zeke.' Jessamyne knew that the more he was after something, the more he had to work up the introductory pitch first.

'I need a partner.' He was trying to smile fondly at her.

'Me? Or y' want my intro to somebody specific… special skills?'

Zeke glanced round to check no-one had drifted within earshot. 'You'll do fine again. Very much on the SN… *Say Nowt*. Besides, me and you… you know?'

She nodded, 'That's understood, course.' Sure enough – they were on-off lovers, every single time they did a job together. Always with as much rancour as rapture. 'Long as you're dead straight with me – I mean it, Zeke. *No tricks.* Not this time. *Never again.* Don't say I didn't warn you.'

'Yeah, yeah. I did the surface mineralogical survey, ten years back. It showed the broadest spread of rare earth elements since Ytterby. I surveyed it on my own, so nobody else knew then, and they still don't. It's absolutely genuine – nothing seeded; nothing fixed. There's yttrium, of course, and ytterbium; erbium and terbium; along with holmium, thulium and gadolinium. Just traces, mind you. And lots of platinum that I found in a massive crevasse that surveyed out as penetrating 72% deep into the rock. The platinum's concentrated there in very minable amounts and purities. The raries are exceptionally good vein amounts deep in there, too. I've never come across any deposits to touch them.'

She's looking interested, he decided, *but hasn't leapt at me enthusiastically.* 'Come on, Jess, rare earth minerals are scarce as jelly on Jupiter in easily-extracted quantities and locations.'

'Sure, but down the bottom of a crevasse is not easily-minable. Certainly not by a beginner at actual ore extraction. Like you.' She thought about it, 'You could have sold that info to Metallics, or AstroMines Inc for a fortune; straight away, complete with percentage and registration rights, and location. That's what we do – survey, sell, and move on.' She withdrew her hand from his stroking touch. 'We're not miners, Zeke.'

'Until now. The thing about this one – Finora, I call it – was the probably-impending collision. I'm the only person who's realised that. It's still not on the official Impending collisions calc tables. If the impact did happen, then Finora would most likely split open at the crevasse site, and I'd be able to survey and extract the minerals so much easier. If the veins stay as rich as they seem, deep inside, then mining'll be a doddle.'

'So you're truly figuring on working it y' self? They're never going to like that, Astro and Metallics.'

'Course they're not, *if* they find out. That's where you come in. I need a partner in getting everything set up. I've been doing the prelim stuff for the past two-fifty days, since I confirmed the collision will definitely happen. It's near time now, Jess. Eleven days. If y' with me, we go now. If y' not, I'll say no more and talk to Mollia.'

'Mo? You're not serious?' *Can't have Mollia getting in the vac-sack with Zeke. Yes… look at his crafty eyes; he knows that, which is the only reason he's mentioned her.* 'I'd be Full Partner? How's that gonna work, then?'

'Tell you on the way there, if you're in.'

All his assurances half-convinced her that he was either being honest about this, or better at lying than he used to be. Still untrusting, but hooked, she nodded, 'All the way, as long as you're straight with me this time, Zeke.'

'No more answers till we're well out into the Belt, and no communication with anyone.'

Zeke's craft, the Mary Darlene, was clearly straight out the scrap orbit. Except that the interior and ion-plus motor had been heavily modified from defunct military vessels. Its scorched and battered appearance belied the reality of a rugged, reliable workshop.

'She has ample cargo capacity for samples, and she don't leak. So no complaints, huh?'

A day checking stores and ship systems, and they drifted away from Tharsis Hub at a tangent to the course they actually required, and plotted in a series of course changes to take over the next six days.

'I carried on registering my surveying interest in eight asteroids every year; that's my usual quota. That meant I had exclusive rights to them for three years. Then I had to submit my surveys, or forfeit the fee. Beacons on each one to warn others off, of course. Then, once I'd talked myself into believing the collision would happen, I also bought five of the nine that I'd checked out the previous year, and four from the year before – the others had already been bought by various operations that usually pay for my reports. The idea was to dilute any unwanted interest in Finora. Make it look like I've taken to buying a few each year – nothing special.

'I never bought a stroid before – I'm a surveyor, for Tarvos' sake – but I wanted to make'em believe I was branching out. You know how the mining oppers are always sniffing round, ready to jump in somewhere.'

'The two big boys monitor *everybody*, Zeke, and most likely know exactly what you're up to – spreading a diversion for something you've discovered. They'll still have somebody watching you on and off. Now, then, when's this stroid collision due to take place?'

'Well, we got plenty of time to... er... you know... *re-acquaint...*'

On the way to sector V909, and Finora in particular, they re-acquainted frequently, and resignedly moaned about the state of affairs in the surveying, prospecting, extraction and transportation industry. Or Belting, as it was generally known.

'Yeah, the regional governance bodies – The Alcades – try to safeguard the rights of us prospectors and surveyors as well as actual miners.' Zeke lolled in the auto-pilot seat, Jess astride him. 'I dunno, most try to be honest in their admin and judicial duties, but there's too much conflict between Whole-belt law and SS Common laws.'

'Especially over which body has precedence in which particular aspect and region,' she agreed, and fiddled at something lower down. 'So many loopholes to be exploited or hidden in; and communications're often subject to breakdown, alteration and misinterpretation—'

'Yeah, deliberate more than accidental. We gotta be on our guard, Jess. *Whoa!* Careful there.'

'It's not like claim jumpers get screwed down when they're caught – only charged with trespass, and allowed to keep any loot they've managed to thieve before being discovered.'

Zeke humphed in a smile, 'Often, the Alcades and their so-called enforcers turned a blind eye—'

'Half of'em are paid by Met or Astro.'

'Or doing it for themselves on the side.'

'I prefer it astride to on the side,' she grinned. 'All that reinterpretation of rights of citizens of the Out-Belt sectors, Jovian Mooners, Inners, Earth miners – didn't help in the least. Made it more tangled for the crooks to hide among the regs. Even I know that much.

'Now, are we getting on with this, before I re-check the coordinates of the next way-point?

Zeke knew it all, living in the dregs of it for the past half of his life: 'It's always the officially re-cog companies versus little men, with or without licences and certificates. Us lot in the middle get the square end every time. If you're one of the small operatives, you have to beware of theft of minerals and equipment; destruction and mislaying of deliveries. There's even been disappearances of complete ships and their cargoes.

'Now and again, one of us little guys reports supplies vanishing, claims polluted, or supplies can't be ordered for some undisclosed reason – and what support do we get? Effall.

'What I find is that your likelihood of becoming a victim depends on which shyker's got their eyes on you.'

In truth, after an especially passionate experiment in null gravity with the rotors on full gain, Zeke and Jessamyne agreed that the great majority of people in the Belt are honest and hard-working, with a good sense of what's right. People worked hard, and life was dangerous. But the money could be good – there wasn't any real need to thieve and kill. The hub and tub centres might be pits of iniquity, but the working belters were sober and safe – in the main.

'Basically,' they panted, 'It's the effin greed of two huge corporations that practically own the Belt—'

'And a few of the middle-sized enterprises.'

'Between'em, they're at the bottom of *all* the crookery around the Belt and Moons regions.'

'Mmm. Fancy another go at the centrifuge?'

The Mary Darlene's crew of two made three additional course changes to confuse any trackers, and did a slingshot around Jupiter. They arrived at the Finora rockball in six days, well in time for the impending collision of asteroids.

'I got half a dozen orbiting cams to send in close to capture the details pre-, peri- and post-collision, and collect all the trajectory data for whatever broken chunks are created and go spinning off. We're not gonna lose a trillion in ore just cos we didn't log one little fragment that went walkies.'

Between episodes of ardour, Zeke explained and demo'd his plans and preps. 'We get on pretty well, eh, Jess?'

'Sure do. Nobody else'd put up with either of us; each as wugged-up as the other, eh?' She stroked, temporarily-fondly over his lean form.

'Always have been, mmm? Now – are we gonna do that one more time, before Finora meets up with Three-twenty-one?'

'Mmm; let's just make sure we've got all this lot set right, huh?' She turned to the sets and screens, 'Let's see – the edi-cams need re-feeding like… *this*, every eight minutes. And redirecting the zooms needs doing one minute in four with *this*, and *here*. That right? Yeah?' She turned back to his space-toughened body, 'Here we go again, then.'

'Which of us is going to be Finora this time, hmm?'

Four... three... two...

'Look at that...'

To the two observers, it wasn't Three-twenty-one colliding with Finora, so much as Finora catching up with the larger body and striking it at an oblique angle – seventy-two degrees. In reality, they simply came together – and parted again.

The result was that Finora split into two major segments and eleven very minor ones that sailed off at speed. Their trajectories were tracked and recorded before Zeke and Jessamyne turned their close attention to Fin and Ora – one twice the size of the other, and split apart perfectly down the great fissure. It had seemed like a slow-motion bump, but there was tremendous force involved – expended mostly in the velocity of the splinters, and some heat. Patches of the major pieces glowed for a time, but not enough to stop the hovercams re-surveying Finora's two main remnants.

Quietly elated, Zeke went over the detail of the wealth with his partner. It was looking like a minimum of a hundred billion in raw visible and projected material.

'So accessible. Some of those veins are the richest I've ever seen – ever heard of, in fact.' They ran the recorders, the whole gamut of analytics.

'If these veins penetrate as deep as your first projections suggested, there could be a trillion here, Zeke. This's mind-shaking stuff.'

They hugged and went over it all again… and again. Embedded their beacons on each major piece, and chased after all the smaller fragments, finding a couple of them were worth keeping ownership beacons on, and dropping simple warning beacons on the others.

'We have to do that to reduce the chances of anyone coming across them unawares. Collisions out here are expensive.

'Not that the rights beacons do all that much good if somebody's determined,' he sighed. 'Metallica and AstroMines have both been caught knocking beacons out, burning them out, stealing them and dropping them onto barren rocks. Overwriting the message claims…'

'Yeah, there was Josey and Chuck I used to work with. She disappeared and he got his mind half-wiped.'

'Similar with Yammer and them other two that set up in the Farside group – they vanished for a year after they turned down a meagre offer from Astro.'

'And a partnership that set up to mine somewhere in the Trojans; they got waylaid, all their equipment wrecked, supplies stolen. Had to sell out to pay their creditors.'

'Well, it's not happening to us, Jess. I'm going to seed our two big chunks.'

'Seed'em? What with? They don't need seeding any more – they're rich as Aunt Fabby. You can't afford enough of these elements to seed them with anything like enough to make a difference. What good would it do?'

'Nukes, Jess. I've got four forty-meg nukes to seed Fin and Ora with. I'm going to rig'em to the beacons, with boobies and timers as well as trips. Anybody tries to steal these babies from us, they're gonna *so* regret it.'

'Shit on Charon, Zeke! You can't do that! It'd melt everything – ruin it all for decades. Could spread... You *can't* do that.'

'Yep, we can, and we will.' He stood, in no mood for argument over this. 'No need for them to go off if we get dealt with right. Come on. You're gonna help me set'em up.'

'Zeke, I can't do that! Illegal doesn't even begin— It's *wrong.*' Horrified, she really meant it. 'Zeke, you're joining the opposition with tactics like this. You *can't* booby-trap them with nuclear weapons. I'm not being part of your mass murder and pollution game.'

'They're not cheating us like they have all the others, Jess. It's simple sense – if they leave us alone, they won't get hurt. Now, come on. I can't manage this on my own. I need you in here to calibrate them while I set them in. You need to monitor me on the data screens and check on the settings when I prime them... *Don't argue, Jess!* You've *got* to do it. Or I'll... I'll dump you out there with the equipment pod. Now – come on. It should take us a day, at most.

'You do it, Jess, or I dump you. Remember that.'

A mass of resistance and seething resentment, Jessamyne did what she had to do, making all the settings, and going over all the readouts as Zeke set the nukes. And, totally resentful, she did it right. *He'd know if I effed it up. Lying maniac shyker.*

It took twelve hours non-stop monitoring the on-going readings and summary analyses while Zeke was outside. The nukes would work, alright. On top of the all-too-immediate threat of being stranded on a rockball with nuclear weapons, she doubly resented Zeke checking her tap-ins. *I suppose it was obvious that he would do that, to make sure I hadn't put any cancel-timers in.*

'Bar steward,' she muttered. 'You can go off folk, you know.'

From being the easy-going, getting-along couple they started out as – all hope and strokes – it all boiled over on the way back to Hildaria Three-Seven to register their newly-confirmed claims in person, attesting to the zipped-in details with a host of images and data streams. Still enraged with the nuclear option, Jessamyne couldn't let it rest, bringing the subject up at five-minute intervals, and threatening every form of retaliation under the sun.

'Shut the shit up, Jess! I'm sick of it. Here – have y' base-rate pay-out and you can scrugg off when we get in. Here... See? *That* was your contract – temporary employee. We ain't partners any more.'

Unbelieving, Jess watched the screen as her partnership contract vanished in the symbolic ball of flame.

'Go on. You're out. I'll finish this off myself. And y' can't do anything about it, cos I still got the over-contract which binds you to me and this enterprise. You should have read it, at least. You know me well enough by now. So it's fully binding. Go on. Get out, and take y' softie-shite morals with you.'

Impotently enraged, there was nothing for her to do except swallow it. The contract had been a non-binding mockery, he claimed. 'Be satisfied with the payout; that's good money for a few deccas work. See you around some time, eh?'

Throughout her next contract period – a deep survey private enterprise on Europa – she nursed her hatred for him, and for her own stupidity in trusting him. But picked up a second-grade report on the work for BeeMines and realised she had to put Zeke behind her. 'Can't afford to get another bad mark. Deserved that one, I did. Must concentrate; do better, girl,' she told herself sternly. *Bit of luck, you'll never see him or hear of him again.*

Buried in her work – a long trip out into Saturn's moons, surveying a promising-looking sector of Herschel Crater on Mimas. Another extended session on Hyperion straight after Mimas, and an independent one along a section of the Halo Ring round Jupiter. It was just about long enough to get the treachery of Zeke out her system. Within, the rage was still simmering, with underbreath cursing whenever he crossed her mind.

'We could have been great, Zeke, you shyker.'

<hr>

It would have to be the Carstairs Lounge, Earth Orbit Four, wouldn't it? Happened to be laid over during an eleven-day routine repair and maintenance booking on her own survey vessel, with little to do. Mooching; not keen on dropping down onto the surface. Too much gravity bother and formalities for only a few days down there.

A touch on her shoulder, a murmur behind her…

'You.' Dead inside, she turned away from a sylo-snatch game on the main table.

'Yep. It's me, Jess.' There, in the flesh and silver lamé, drink in hand, broad smile.

The sight was enough to stop her heart. 'Scrugg off, Zeke, you bastard. You wrecked me.'

'I know, I know. It's been doing the same for me, Jess. I came specially – knew you'd be here. Can you sit awhile? It's been a long time – three hundred days tomorrow, by my calcs.'

'What's to talk about? You let me down, kicked me out. I must'a been so stupid to trust you.' She shook her head as she succumbed to sitting with her former bed-and-business partner. 'Going to rub it in, huh?'

'Here, Jess.' He passed a slide-sheet to her. 'That's the original contract – equal rights with all partners. That's still yours, still valid. And it's registered at C'n'C in Hildaria Offices. Go on, read it. It's registered on Earth Central. And SS Common Office. I never flamed it. Just a pretence, Jess.'

She finished her drink, tapped for another, and read the screen-out. Looked at him. 'What in four moons are you up to, Zeke?'

'Have your drink, Jess. Come on. I insist.'

'I'll stick with the intikam fruit.' She waved the fruit knife under his nose. 'So stay back.'

'Okay, okay, you keep the contract whatever, but if you listen, you'll know why. Then go or stay as you wish – on whatever basis you fancy,' he gazed at her hopefully. 'Yeah? Okay?'

She nodded, resentment teetering on boiling over as her eyes flickered over the contract, determined to read this one properly. 'You push it too far, Zeke; always have done. I told you at the start – no more.'

'You had to earn it, Jess,' he wheedled. 'I needed you to be absolutely shugged off, and do exactly what you did that first night we got back. Everything was fake – except you. You – absolutely genuine. You were the front guy; our window... image to the worlds.

'The two guys in the bar? After we split, and you went off on a splender in the dokie bars? Yeah, the ones you ranted and raved with. Pumped you up a bit, did they? Going on about my nukes and what a scrugging cheating rock-sucker I am. You were great,' he laughed, finishing his drink.

'You had to do it right, Jess. You were being followed: they were agents from Astro. Plus three, we think, from Metallica. It wasn't thio-guns they had on you: it was micro-poly monitors. You *had* to be telling the truth. The truth as you understood it. They even got hold of my recordings to check the nukes – verified everything you said, and more besides. If you hadn't totally believed it, they would have known.

'Now come on, Jess, don't be like this. You haven't starved, have you? The pay-out we gave you was pretty good for two-dozen days' work, wasn't it? Just regard it as a small bonus, eh?'

She looked up from the contract, 'What's all this "we", Zeke?'

'Ah, yes... You remember Yammer, who we worked with out at Ryugu? and the brothers who disappeared at the same time? Yeah, well, we pooled our resources and were intending to seed a rock in Four-X Inner Zone. Then Finora came up. Yes, I really did buy it, but the survey only showed normal levels of rare earths – good on platinum, though. And Three twenty-one was going to miss. Not by much, but definitely wouldn't collide.'

He tried to smile reassuringly, and reached to her hand. She pulled it well clear of him, looking more inclined to spike him with the fruit knife at the least excuse.

'Eh? I saw them collide – we chased the bits. We put the beacons out... Fin and Ora.' Caught between disbelief and bafflement, Jess blustered.

'Now what's all this "we" Jess? It wasn't "we" who went down – it was me, alone. Sure I went down, onto a still-intact Finora. The rest? All simulations that cost a fortune. Yammer and the Rofferty brothers created sim readings and analyses; screen-outs. Everything was faked. You had to totally believe it.'

'I still do. I saw it. I helped you.' He wasn't going to smarm his way back into her favour in a hurry.

'Indeed – just not how you think. Your greatest role was in getting drunk and letting your mouth run off with you. So predictable.'

'So... So?' She checked through the last section of the contract again.

Zeke was smug, smiling. 'They came looking for me, so I confessed all down at Central Records, and told'em I was terrified of being got at by Metallica and AstroMines. I showed'em a ton of records about Astra's threats and Metallica's actual crimes against Central reps and officers. So the officials there weren't going to let anything happen to me. I was their biggest witness in the case they're mounting.'

'Like I said, Zeke, *So?*'

'So Astro and Met both made offers, and pitched against each other for rights to the non-existent Fin and Ora, plus all the bits. And to know the codes for the nukes. And for me to lose the evidence against their people – which was mostly invented, anyway, but there must have been an awful lot of truth in it to bother them that much.

So they paid me off – Paid *us* off. Four partners – Me, you, Yammer... and the Roffertys count as one share. It's around eighteen billion each, all told.'

'Zeke,' she was renewed in her horror. 'You can't. You'll never get away with it. They'll be after you in no time. And me.'

'No, they won't. They've had long enough; I've been available and they haven't moved. Embarrassed, maybe. Or can't quite figure out what went wrong. They probably still can't quite believe it's happened.'

'So now?' Jessamyne was trembling as she re-read all the noughts on the mini-screen alongside her contract; studied the tiny-print again; looked at him doubtfully.

'We got choices, Jess. Forgive me, and come with me – we're made for each other – best team in the SS. Always have been.'

'Where to?' Buried in suspicion, she wasn't going to let Zeke get close again, not in any sense. Not so easy.

'I was thinking, maybe Ganymede. There's a quadrant unclaimed where we could do the same with Jovian Mining Inc. Or,' he saw the look on Jess's face. 'Or, we could head down onto Earth. I bought an island. It has thousands of palm trees, and beaches by the dozen. And nuke missiles, just in case.'

'Sounds wonderful,' beaming, she slid across, next to him, wondering, just for a second, *What do you have planned for me there?* She dismissed the fleeting thought and snuggled close against him.

Two seconds later, her fruit blade was deep between his ribs and twisting violently.

'Jess? Wha—? They got at you? *Jeez, Jess...*'

The blade went in again, lacerating his right lung. 'Not them, Zeke. *You.* You should'na done that to me. I told you to be dead straight with me. I warned you I'd kill you. And I just read the bit in the contract where it says, "...equally shared among *surviving* members of the partnership." With you gone, I get an extra six billion for what you put me through.'

A few notes

Purely because I like the sound of my own keyboard, I thought I'd finish up by saying – there's no telling where stories are going to come from.

The most common sources of stories are:
1. Almost daily walks around Brinsley and surrounding villages, with a mind freed-up from the computer;
2. Soaking in the bath with little more than a navel to contemplate;
3. Sitting in the afternoon summer sun, in the garden, by the ponds, with a shandy to set the biro blazing across the page.
4. In a car park practically anywhere because I've arrived early for an appointment, and somebody won't let me sit inside.
5. A chance remark or situation on the net or the telly, and I think, "If that was in a million years' time, a million light years away…"

- The Fattest Backside arose from overhearing someone at the bar, and I thought he'd be in an awful mess if his missus heard him. Unless…
- Warphans came from a telly programme about the orphans of war in Africa. On both sides, the children all looked the same – miserable. And I just thought, "What the eff are their parents fighting with each other about, with that as the only result?"
- Continuum began on a tour of volcanoes in Indonesia, and I was struck by the huge, ancient churches and temples that abound there; half of them derelict and

overgrown; others very well used by many of the populace.
- Chits came to me on a fly-drive round the western states, USA. Such old mining towns aren't uncommon, boasting a single main street, dust devils and old-timers nowadays.
- Kaleidoscope occurred to me when watching glass ornaments being made and shaped in the furnace, with a variety of colours in beautiful shapes, and chatting with the artists.
- The Emperor's New Clothes originated in Heathrow airport, with the fan-fared arrival of some over-dressed dignitary in his flowing gold and multi-coloured clothes and his equally gaudily-dressed entourage. I thought it was time someone toned him down.
- Me, the Prof and a Tail to Tell – The times we've been uncovering some large fossil – usually a dinosaur footprint, or row of them – and wondered how far the associated evidence of its environment would spread – the mud splatter, plants pressed aside, raindrops, tail drag, other footprints… Who knows what we might uncover?
- Just Some Old Guy: I see the old guys (Old? They're younger than me, most of them) collecting their pension or morning papers, taking the dog for a walk, or calling for a pint, and I think, "There really must be a lot more to you than meets the eye".
- I'm Not Perfect Yet came from the hundreds of times I inspected schools of all kinds, and it was always expected that I would understand their whole *raison d'être* in advance. I tried very hard, but there was no pleasing some of them. Suppose I hadn't even tried?

- Choices – a mix of my younger brother's tales of bars around the world where merchant sailors go for a ~~riot~~, er, a drink; and my own recollections of a few people very much out of place in such environments.
- A Bit Bigger. Jaws, of course.

I have probably another three or four hundred stories jotted down – from half a page to twenty pages, whether longhand in notebooks, or rough-typed on a laptop or mobile phone. Perhaps half of them will see the light of day if I can keep going long enough. There are some I'm dying to complete, but can't quite get the end right. And a few where the middle escapes me. So frustrating, but time will tell.

Ciao, Trevor W

The Author and his Books

Trevor is a Nottinghamshire, UK writer. Educated at Old Basford Primary School, Nottingham; High Pavement Grammar School, Nottingham; Hull University, and Nottingham University.

His short stories and poems have frequently won prizes, and he has appeared on television discussing local matters.

As well as New-Classic Sci-Fi and the OsssOss Series of short stories, he has published many reader-friendly non-fiction books and articles. These are mostly about exploring active volcanoes around the world, and searching for fossilised dinosaur footprints on Yorkshire's Jurassic coast. The portrait photograph was taken in a fossil quarry at Solnhofen, Germany.

In the 1980s, his Ph.D. research pioneered the use of computers in the education of children with profound learning difficulties. Much of this research was published in educational, medical and computing magazines and journals.

He spent fourteen years at the classroom chalkface; sixteen as headteacher of a special school; and sixteen as an Ofsted school inspector to round it off. At the time, his teacher wife, Chris, joked that it was "Sleeping with the Enemy".

Now retired, he writes, walks the local footpaths, curses his computers, and loves his wife, the cat and his kids.

OsssOss Books

The Odds, Sods and Surprises Series of Short Stories

TreVor WaTTs Sci-Fi Collection

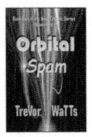

Short Stories

Coming soon

New-Classic Sci-fi

Realms of Kyre

Medieval Fantasy Saga from the Inside – from the intimate to the world-shattering

A badly injured stranger is discovered in the forest swamp, seemingly fallen from an empty sky.

With no memory of who he is, or awareness of the hidden powers he holds, why must he battle against roving bandits, invading forces, and even the troopers who found him, and called him Kyre? What choice does he have about combat in the arena? Will he always surrender to the whims and commands of the lord? and the wiles and demands of the women who slide into his bed?

As he struggles to survive and discover who and what he is, how does his fate become entangled with the destiny of the Five Realms?

Books 1 and 2 due for publication in 2022

Realms of Kyre

Book 1: Foundling
Chapter 1. That's how it works

'Jackto! Get your squad together. You're doing a lancing patrol into the forest.'

Sub Jackto and his half-dozen troopers stared at Bannerman Mink.

'Now?'
      'In this heat?'
           'Whafor?'

'Not scheduled.' They all had something to say.

'Just fryking do it! Captain's orders. Look. See her? Over where the forids are tethered?

The group looked: a woman, not in swamp green uniform. 'So?'

'She's Rua. *The Sisterhood.*'

They looked again. 'Is that Captain Briand she's with?

'The Sisters, huh? Never seen one before.'

'In an army camp? What's her sort doing here?

'Never mind her reasons. She sensed something. "A powerful presence," she told Briand. Look, Jackto, *she* said it. Captain believed it; or at least surrendered to it – you've heard of the Rua: they have influence. *He* ordered me to send a squad to investigate. *I* pass it to you. So *you* go and check it out. That's how it works, remember?'

'Where? There's a dozen days of rotting forest swamp out there.' Jackto waved beyond the camp's palisade walls towards the dense, seemingly endless spread of treetops.

'Straight between here and the tall pinday tree. *That* one,' Mink pointed. 'She gets a mind impression of something *different*; beyond her understanding, she says – about two thirds of the way.'

'It'll be a good two hours getting there.'

Complaining routinely, the troopers began collecting their weapons, accepting their lot.

'It's deep swamp that far out.' One tried a final protest. 'Stinking hot and sparse on trails.'

'You'll have to get a move on then, won't you?'

Waving Jackto and the platform of troopers away, Bannerman Mink sighed, *Better not mention the other thing the captain told me – That Rua woman also said the sudden appearance of this presence in the swamp had torn the weft of the Realm. I don't imagine that bodes well for anyone.*

Chapter 2. The swamp stirred

Instant blinding awareness from nothing. Stabbing pain.

Kyre ruk! What is this? Where am I?

Gasping to breathe, the thing struggling in the pit of endless, heavy mud was close to panic. Mouth and nose blocked with slime, he knew he was sinking, drowning.

Flashes of bright sun, and falling, spun in his mind.

Something writhed in his throat, driving out his flickering thoughts of sky and tumbling. Gagging at the foulness of the squirming thing within, his fingers clutched, couldn't reach. Retching on the taste and the stench, his body convulsed.

A memory of smashing through branches and leaves was there for a beat, then gone, as a splat of mud dropped into his face. A glance up – a broken tree branch, still dripping mud.

Sinking deeper, already exhausted, the man-like creature realised its struggles were making things worse. 'Need to stop. Let the pain ease; strength return. *Kyre hresh?* What's happened? Where am I? What are these crawling things?'

A pan-head worm began to fix its teeth into his skin; a swarm of sangui insects hovered closer.

Wait; not fight…

Rest; try to remember…

Fading to blackness…

***

Suddenly aware again, the captive of the mire shuddered violently, scattering the cloud of brilliant red and green insects away from the bloodied, open gash in his head. Scarcely breathing in a world of glooping mud and shrill, zipping insects, he struggled to remember, 'Who am I? *Ky-toin?* What the *fryke* has happened to me?'

A single weak, choking cough escaped him; not enough to be rid of the worm that slowly squirmed in his throat. What am I? Is this pain I feel? I know nothing of pain; and yet, I feel it here as much as the mud.

Think back; I *must* know who I am, where I am. Why am I here?

Wait…

Wait… Was I falling?

Darkness settled in him again.

***

Voices! Loud and close! Crashed into his mind.

'It's a man. Brigand got himself in a mess—'

'Hill bandit.'

'Gerrim ahter there!'

'He's stark bollock.' A voice so loud. So close.

'Gerrold ovim!'

'Stop struggling y' cunny.' Voices so raucous.

Forcefully grasped, he was jolted to new awareness.

'Wha's appnin...?' as he was dragged through steaming mud, branches and leaves, legs trailing, kicking feebly.

Slimed and bloodied, he was dumped naked, sitting on a rotting log. 'He can't breathe. Check his mouth and throat. Thump his back.'

Kuit! This is me? This convulsing body?

'Come on, lads, get him breathing. Clean him up. See what we got under all the mud.'

Need to cough... can scarce breathe. Men hitting my back. Shouting, laughing all around me.

Black mud spurted out his mouth; blood splattering down him. He tried to reach to his side, where the flesh was split open in a huge rip, flesh straining out, a mud-worm squirming within, sinking back.

Can't stop shaking. Covered in blood.

'That's it. Got him breathing.'

His breath began to rasp almost steadily as he coughed and gasped, becoming aware of hard faces and drawn swords around him. Sweat-soddened men in muddied, dull-green uniforms, staring at him in disbelief.

This is all so wrong, not what should be happening. This whole place reeks of decay.

'You're soldiers? Who are you? *Kyre vriy?* You odious creatures?'

In some awful guttural language, they demanded and sneered; laughed and poked at him, asking; pointing up into the trees, at broken branches. Huge splatters of mud adorning drapes of grey lichen.

'Me? I fell through the trees? Where the *kuit* from?'

***

A pair of troopers closed round him, peering and prodding at his head, muttering. 'Fryking head's split open, Sub. He ain't gonna last long.'

Unaware, he muttered in return. '*Kyre rej?* What's wrong up there?' and reached up. Cursed, '*Fryke!*' as he discovered the jagged gash in his skull.

One of the men, a scar across his face, grunted, and jerked his hand away. Then splashed swampy water over his head, and began to tease fragments away, showing the swamp-man splinters of bone and wood. Their eyes met; both grimaced.

'*Yye froik.* That doesn't look good. Bone. And wood splinters?' He stared disbelievingly at the bone fragments. My head's shattered? I'm finished before I started. Started what? *Why am I here?*

Some of the men jabbered, pointing at his eyes. 'See there? Eyes sparking like fire.'

'From The Pit, is he?'

'My eyes? What about them? *Gahi Kyre?*'

One forced his fingers into the prisoner's mouth, clawing, tugging out a long, flat-headed worm. Two more were painfully prised from his skin. The troopers poked and dug in distaste at his side, where the flesh was torn apart, fingers grasping at another writhing creature deep within.

Trying to force the pain away, he demanded, *'Na Kyre?* What do you want? Who are you?'

No-one answered. Baffled shrugs from them. More incomprehensible muttering and head-shaking. One raised a sword over him. 'He's a Pit demon; we should get rid of him. Dump him back in there.'

Scarface pushed the blade away, rapping orders, 'Bannerman Mink wants him. So does the captain.'

A rope slipped round the naked man's neck.

'Kyre ruki? What are you doing?' He grabbed at it, protesting, Too slow; too feeble, he was dragged upright, swaying, gazing blankly at dark-misted trees draped with hanging, mud-splattered growths. A crater of mud; filthy brown-green water oozing back into it; a few faint wraiths of steam rising. *I fell? From where?* Blue sky showed through a gap in the trees.

One trooper snapped an order.

Another nodded, sheathing his sword. 'Whatever you say, Jackto.'

The prisoner was forced away with a sword thrust and a jerk on the neck rope.

'Kyre reshi?' he mumbled. 'Where are you taking me? What for?'

…continued in eBook and Paperback.